I0445868

Lies In Progress

Also by Stanley Goldstein

Fiction
Park West: A Novel of Love and Murder and Redemption

Nonfiction
Troubled Children/Troubled Parents

STANLEY GOLDSTEIN

Lies In Progress

WYSTON BOOKS, INC.

WYSTON BOOKS, INC.
P.O. Box 1280
Warwick, NY 10990-1280

Tel.: (845) 986-6888
E-mail: askus@wystonbooks.com
Please visit our Website: *www.wystonbooks.com*

This is a work of fiction. Names, characters, places and incidents are the product of the author's imagination or used fictitiously. Any resemblance to actual events, locations, or persons, living or dead, is coincidental.

Publisher Cataloging-in-Publication Data

Goldstein, Stanley
Lies in progress: a novel/Stanley Goldstein
Includes bibliographical references

1.Teenage Girls Fiction
2. Terrorism Fiction
3. United States Political History Fiction

Library of Congress Control Number: 20021000705

813'.6—DC21

ISBN 978-0-9717705-1-5 (Print Edition)
ISBN 978-0-9717705-6-0 (E-book edition)

Cover photographs by: (1) Lilli Day/Photodisc Collection (2) Visions of America/Joe Sohm/Photodisc Collection Both licensed from Getty Images

Copyright © 2002, 2010 by Stanley Goldstein.
All rights reserved.
Printed on acid free paper.

To the late Harriet Pilpel,
my first literary agent

Part of us is claimed by our country,
part by our parents,
part by our friends.
—Roman Proverb

I HEARD a voice, that cried,
"Balder the Beautiful
Is dead, is dead!"
—Longfellow, *Tegner's Drapa*

CONTENTS

Author's Note

THIS IS A work of fiction. If you believe a character to be someone that you know, trust me you don't. But publicized historical events and, unfortunately, the science and mechanics of terrorism, are accurately described.

Lies In Progress was completed just days before the attacks on New York City and Washington, these making necessary minor descriptive changes. Hopefully, government actions will cause the weapon described in this book to remain fanciful.

I thank my brother, Leonard, for his long support and helpful suggestions.

Comments are welcome.

Stanley Goldstein

Hudson Valley, New York

November, 2001

Website: *www.drstanleygoldstein.com*

E-mail: drstan@drstanleygoldstein.com

Author's Note to the Digital Edition

IT HAS BEEN nine years since I completed writing *Lies In Progress*. Since then, little has changed with regard to terrorism. The threat still exists though, thankfully, the event described as CATACLYSM in this book has not occurred. Hopefully, with enough luck and vigilance, it never will.

While editing this edition, correcting a few typos from the printed version and changing occasional words and punctuation marks, I again became riveted by the experiences of LeeAnn and The Major: a teenager confronting greater peril than anyone should; and a deeply flawed man seeking redemption. I hope that your emotions will be equally stirred too.

As always, comments are welcome.

Stanley Goldstein
Hudson Valley, New York
November, 2010

Website: www.drstanleygoldstein.com
E-mail: drstan@drstanleygoldstein.com

FOREWORD

THE TV NEWS droned on as he explained my poisoning. Torn refugees and smartly dressed soldiers; then an eleven year old baton twirler whose loose costume anticipated my diminishing curves.

Later we viewed a documentary of the husband who disposed of his wife's body fragments in a stream. Hopefully she was dead before chipping began. If guidelines for lovers still exist *that* should be the first!

Or is murder now acceptable when a great political career is at stake? When certain things must simply be done and not considered.

BOOK ONE

LOVE, AND AFTER

Beginnings

CHAPTER ONE

"**H**IS THING WAS BIG AND HAIRY."

"Well aren't they?"

"Some," her friend responded with a knowing smile. Not laughing since their geometry teacher, though he was in his sixties, wasn't yet deaf or unobservant. Both girls stared intently onto their worksheets with lips barely moving.

"What else?"

"You can read it," the seventeen year old said to her younger classmate, passing the letter across the small space separating their desks.

It was four pages and was written in a stream of consciousness style as if the writer had been trying both to communicate and to understand her experience.

"We met in Media Play's parking lot after work. He asked if I was hungry and I said that I didn't eat since lunch and he said that he had food in his City apartment but never learned how to cook and I said that I could. We went in separate cars and he drove fast so I had to drive fast too which scared me but I was more scared of losing him.

"He was smoking when I parked but put the cigarette out when he saw me—I HATE smoking. But it doesn't seem to matter so much when you're in love. Maybe he knows how I feel and is trying to stop smoking.

His apartment is on East 50th Street by the river. The doorman smiled like he wondered if I was his daughter or his niece but I smiled as if I belonged there which maybe now I do.

"The apartment has two entrances: one into a small foyer and the other through the kitchen. The refrigerator and stove are old fashioned and he said that he was lent the apartment by a friend and didn't change anything since he only sleeps there when he works late and his wife never comes. I guess he noticed that I felt funny when he said wife cause he put his arm round me and I felt warm and the funny feeling went away.

Then he said that it was time to feed me and smiled which I love to see and we went to the tiny kitchen and found ham and cheese and bread and he said that we could eat in bed.

"I knew we'd have sex since the first time I felt him hard against me but wondered who does what and when? But everything went easy! He said it's fun showering together and I smiled and said OK but I had to pee and he said I should and I did and then I called him into the bathroom and we took off our clothes and went into the shower and he soaped me and I soaped him and his thing was big and hairy. Mom coming. More tomorrow."

The sixteen year old slipped the note back.

"Seeing LeeAnn tonight?"

"I'll be at her house on Friday—come!"

"I'm baby-sitting but call me!"

Her friend agreed and both looked up into the scowl of their teacher, feeling relief when he didn't demand to see the note. Twenty minutes later school was over and the girls walked to their Scarsdale homes, deep in conversation and barely acknowledging passing friends.

"Where did they meet?"

"He needed someone to teach him how to use his computer and her father volunteered her."

"For what?" the grinning sixteen year old asked. In response, she received a painful grip on her shoulder.

"No one knows but you and no one else will!"

Her friend reassured her and their discussion turned to the new, expensive, and little used teen center in this wealthy community. Though formerly a Jewish enclave it now held considerable Christian population, they having been attracted by the excellent schools and manicured fantasy of sobriety. Here, students who worked were motivated by the desire for independence and not poverty.

The Media Play where LeeAnn worked was a factory like cavernous building. Its unfinished beam ceiling enclosed a carpeted area of book, record, and video game displays, armchairs, and snack bar.

Once, at her last job, she sat and aimlessly turned index cards, having finished the available work but being unwilling to leave early and lose pay. Suddenly her shoulder was patted by the smiling boss who said, "doing great." Even Media Play was better.

LeeAnn was barely sixteen but her height (five feet ten inches) and gravity of expression made her seem older. She was quiet and paused before speaking, as if considering spontaneous speech unwise, even dangerous.

Her straight blond hair extended halfway down her back. This seductive element was, however, unmatched by her behavior for she wore no makeup and, her friends insisted, had worn a skirt only twice since kindergarten: for class graduation ceremonies. Yet her persistent concern for others, as reflected in the favors she volunteered, caused no one to doubt her femininity. She was a girl who looked like a woman and thought like the mother she had become for her two younger sisters.

LeeAnn felt guilty. Not about having sex which she felt was her decision to make. But for lying to her parents who believed that she had been working late doing inventory. Even if everyone was asleep when she got home and, as usual, they asked no questions the next day.

Her mother slept late. Her father returned home from work between midnight and three, when their frequent arguments began. These didn't last long since he took the seven fifty train to New York City. LeeAnn wondered how he functioned at his law firm with so little sleep and where he spent his evenings.

The Monsters (her five year old twin sisters—the result of a poorly placed diaphragm after a drunken party her mother once confided) had now chosen their clothes for the first time, in an acceptable but creative fashion. Then they glared at LeeAnn because her lateness made it impossible for her to dress them as she usually did.

Choosing her clothes wasn't a problem: a shirt and jeans. Nor was underwear, a girl in the locker room once suggesting that she could manage with a tight T-shirt instead of a bra. She wasn't really flat but her breasts *were* small. Like her vagina which Ralph liked. Or maybe he just said that he did.

LeeAnn thought how differently women and men related to sex. Only now did the phrase of her friends, "sex starved," make sense. She realized that she had sex because Ralph was understanding. Possibly another man, from some bizarre curiosity, would have insisted that she pee in front of him. But he had sensed the timidity beneath her confident smile and responded to it. Why *had* he wanted her? Not because she was a good lay or from being horny for he could certainly find a more experienced woman with his looks and money and he had a wife.

These thoughts caused her to miss the last step and her books went flying as she grabbed the banister. The Monsters quickly stopped laughing for she hadn't yet made them breakfast.

While driving to school her sisters chatted about their teacher's cupcakes and scary stories. Being good readers and nosy, LeeAnn prayed that they hadn't found her letters.

Despite protests she accompanied them to their classroom though this made her late. No way would she leave them at the building's door as her mother did.

Her first class was English and this teacher didn't comment on lateness, choosing to avoid unnecessary confrontations. Twenty nine years before she had argued about a trivial matter with a teenager who committed suicide the next morning.

Though it was impossible that her words caused this, she thereafter hassled students only about important matters, making her the most popular teacher in the school. Even being voted by a senior class as the one they would most value being marooned with.

She had never married despite the promise of her name (Bea Frootful), this having aroused an insider joke which students affectionately shared with newcomers.

LeeAnn's crotch itched. She squirmed in her seat, hoping that it would help but it didn't, and she wondered if the sex caused it or some disease. Once, after a boy fondled her, she found white spots on her thigh and frantically called Penny who suggested that she wash the soap off.

LeeAnn wondered if she looked different as a non-virgin and smiled as she remembered having once believed that others knew when she was menstruating.

Bored with the class work, a review of grammar for that week's exam, she wrote another note.

"You were right—it didn't hurt. He slept for a few minutes and we had sex again when he woke which was fun but not as much as the first time. I fell asleep and when I woke he was getting dressed so I got dressed and we drove home but slower. I didn't see the doorman which I was glad of and told him. He said that with the size of the Christmas present he gives him he'd better be polite. He kissed me before leaving and said that he'd call me.

"Am I his girlfriend or his sex buddy? Will I teach him computer again and can I be sure what he's paying for now? If for sex, more than thirty dollars I hope! I won't know for weeks: he's going away. More next."

The bell rang and LeeAnn joined the throng surging through the halls. Penny was in her biology class and she would slip her the note to her there.

This teacher, Mr. Haskley, raved at late students, deprecated all, and generated numerous complaints. But he was too near retirement for disciplinary measures to be effective. Decades before, to arouse sympathy, a principal implied that his behavior was caused by a war injury. But the ensuing sympathetic effect soon disappeared as student suffering continued.

LeeAnn's concentration flagged after giving Penny the note. But it momentarily became acute upon hearing the word "insides." Then she had a thought: maybe sex was a deeper experience for women than for men because their body was *invaded* during sex.

The boy behind whispered in her ear, "What would you do if two guys raped you?"

LeeAnn usually ignored dumb comments. Now, realizing the depth of the sexual experience, her response had greater vehemence than she had intended.

"*I'd Bobbitt them*," she replied.

CHAPTER TWO

IT WAS SUNDAY and LeeAnn wanted to sleep until eleven since Media Play opened at noon. Lately she was always tired. But, as usual, The Monsters woke her at six. She was their combination mother/sister/playmate and expected things to stay like this until she was thirty or even later. If (God forbid) her parents had another child she would become a twenty first century spinster, caring for their offspring until...

Even the money she earned wasn't really hers. Her father invested it and she got twenty dollars weekly allowance. At *her* age. Having to ask for money even for underwear. Ugh.

At least today they'd be taking The Monsters out for brunch so she didn't have to make waffles for them. When they first demanded it she stormed, "this isn't a restaurant and you eat what I make." So they refused and, finally, she cooked what they wanted having finally discovered, like all mothers, that it was easier.

Traffic was minimal on I87 and she reached the parking lot before her stomach felt bloated. Again. But it felt better after she peed. She was probably coming down with something. Hopefully not mono which kept Julia out of school for a year. She couldn't imagine her mother caring for *her*.

The afternoon passed quickly as she thought of her last date with Ralph. She had spent an hour teaching him to use his computer so taking money wasn't embarrassing even after they had sex. First on the floor, then "a quickie" as he called it, she straddling him while he sat on the sofa. Though he was her father's age, he was certainly fun. She wondered if things would change after his divorce which he didn't feel free to get until his youngest son was fourteen in three years.

She imagined herself being stepmother to a teenage boy. While being mother to her sisters. And the wife of her father's (*former*) best friend. Then she wondered if Ralph had an affair with her mother. But she quickly dismissed this thought and felt ashamed that she had it though being puzzled why. Maybe because of how her mother glows when speaking his name. But Ralph is good looking, LeeAnn thought.

"Where're the computer books?"

"Second row back from the wall, top shelf."

The customer's question and her assignment to a cash register permanently disrupted this train of thought and she spent the rest of the afternoon worrying about her science project. Then it was early to sleep and up at six. Again.

CHAPTER THREE

LᴇᴇAɴɴ ꜰᴇʟᴛ ʟɪᴋᴇ she was drifting. She smiled and said the right things but wasn't really there. While staring out the window during biology lab, she imagined Ralph inside of her. When the teacher asked what she was thinking she started to say his name, then quickly blurted "rats." Even the teacher laughed. The smell of formaldehyde got to her and she left the room to pee. Afterward, her stomach felt less bloated but still tight.

During gym, LeeAnn lost her balance playing volley ball and fell. She pretended that she twisted her ankle and spent an hour in the nurse's office being mothered. She wanted to stay all day but made the mistake of walking normally while getting juice from the vending machine.

She met Julia during a break.

"What did mono feel like?" LeeAnn asked.

"You're dying. Can barely walk to the bathroom or do anything."

"Think I got it."

"Not if you're here. I was in bed for six weeks. Having to care for a baby."

"What is?"

"What mom said. Who're you going to the prom with?"

"No one. Alone."

"Dennis wants to ask you."

"Please. I remember when he stuck a straw up his nose and talked about farting."

"He's more grown up now and it's time you started dating!"

Her friends' pressure to date was worse this year. If she had guts she would say that she was crazy but then they would threaten to send Valerie the Psycho after her. LeeAnn looked forward to the end of the school day.

While sitting on the stairs waiting for The Monsters, LeeAnn felt about to burst. She had to tell *someone* about Ralph but who? No more to Penny who gossiped. But Valerie was a loner and in the sixth grade had slugged a boy who grabbed LeeAnn's breasts. Which made them the friends they probably still were.

Having decided what to do, LeeAnn closed her eyes and enjoyed the warmth of the sun on her face. While remembering the boy's hands on her breasts, they felt tight. Again.

CHAPTER FOUR

Next day LeeAnn met Julia. Her boyfriend, lacking a condom, had used plastic wrap tied with a rubber band and gobs of the lubricant (VagiNilla Swish) which was sold at the mall. Julia choked with laughter, then looked uncomfortable and said, "You'll know what it's like someday. When you can't keep your hands off a boy." Her face reflected knowledgeable superiority.

LeeAnn smiled wanly and wondered where Valerie was. She went to the school office.

"I borrowed lunch money from Valerie Simnez yesterday and want to pay her back so she's not short. Can I see her schedule?"

After the expected hassling, LeeAnn got the information and walked towards the Earth Science Lab. Valerie had always wanted to be a geologist.

Steeling herself, LeeAnn opened the door to face tables filled with rocks, chemicals, beakers, and a flaming Bunsen burner. But, once there, she didn't know what to say. Thankfully, Valerie waved.

"Don't come close. What brings you here?"

"Dropped off The Monsters early and was wandering."

"Monsters?"

"My five year old sisters."

"Like my seven year old brother. Maybe we could fix him up with one of them."

Their conversation flagged and LeeAnn's intent to tell about Ralph dwindled. She thought to leave and turned, but then began sobbing.

Valerie left her worktable and touched her arm.

"Is it that bad?"

"No." But LeeAnn couldn't stop crying, having been weepy for the previous two days.

"Why me?" Valerie asked. "You must be really alone," she added softly.

"Huh?"

"You avoid me for four years. Then show up where nobody *ever* comes and start bawling. Maybe I should investigate the rocks in your head." But she smiled as she said this and LeeAnn managed a teary grin.

"I always liked you," LeeAnn said.

"*Psycho Val*? That's what they call me isn't it?"

LeeAnn was silent.

"Would it make a difference?" Valerie persisted.

"No," LeeAnn lied. "They'll be calling me that soon."

Valerie's smile was replaced with a concerned frown. Seating herself on a lab bench, she motioned for LeeAnn to sit opposite and considered whether to share more. She remembered once having punching a boy who bothered

LeeAnn: her passivity and naiveté aroused protective instincts in others.

During Valerie's six year relationship with David she had learned to be silent but she needed a friend too. A girl to bounce things off of though knowing that gossip could send David to jail and wreck his career.

Now, for the first time, Valerie risked telling.

"I first had sex at twelve with my nineteen year old cousin. A big secret isolates you."

LeeAnn determined not to appear shocked.

"That's illegal isn't it."

"Many fun things are."

"But with a cousin."

"People think so but it's OK in nineteen states and every European country. We could marry in New York or California though not Pennsylvania. I'd rather be married in Paris than Scranton anyway, wouldn't you?"

LeeAnn stopped crying. She sensed that her instinct to trust Valerie was a good one and vowed to follow it more.

"Do you still see him?" LeeAnn asked.

"When we can. He's pretty busy interning at St. Lukes. Have you had breakfast yet?"

"No. Lately I can't eat in the morning."

"How 'bout chocolate yogurt? It's in the lab refrig for teacher, Honors' students, and guests."

"Chocolate anytime."

While eating, and sensing that LeeAnn was feeling more relaxed, Valerie asked that question the answer to which she already knew since only having sex with a much older guy would cause LeeAnn to fall apart like this. A secret she couldn't trust with chatty girls or her mother. Who was he? Her father? A teacher? Not the janitor she hoped, though he was sexy in a backwoods way. She also wondered if LeeAnn was pregnant or had considered this. Both girls needed a close friend.

"Well?" Valerie asked.

"Well what?"

"Who is he?"

LeeAnn hesitated. Naming Ralph would make their relationship seem too real and her life was already spinning out of control. But classes would start in ten minutes. If she intended to tell, she better do it now. So she did tell, but not his name.

"*Carl*. An old friend of my father."

"Is he married?"

"Has three sons too."

"Good in bed?" Valerie asked with a smile.

"My first. They don't get any better I think."

"The class gets here in a minute and we have to talk. How about after school?"

"I'm working till nine."

"Nine fifteen at the diner?"

"OK, but just for a few minutes. I feel awful tired lately."

Now Valerie felt sure that LeeAnn was pregnant.

CHAPTER FIVE

THEY SAT IN the diner's rear booth. Valerie ordered coffee and LeeAnn ordered hot chocolate. LeeAnn felt better after telling Valerie about Ralph but then regretted it concluding that, as usual, she was tending to backtrack on her decisions. Sensing her discomfort, Valerie started chatting. David planned to be a psychiatrist and said that when you want to talk about something painful it is best to get the other person comfortable first.

"Do you wear thongs?" Valerie asked.

"Just during the summer. My feet get cold."

"Not those, idiot." But Valerie downplayed her criticism with a grin.

Suddenly LeeAnn realized what Valerie meant and blushed, to Valerie's amazement.

"My mom would never pay for 'em."

Valerie concluded if that was LeeAnn's immediate reaction then she must have considered buying them and therefore wasn't as inhibited as she seemed. David would have been proud of this insight.

"Nowadays they sell 'long side TicTacs in Salt Lake City. Even grandmothers buy 'em. David bought me one which laced at the front though you really can't unlace a g-string."

Now LeeAnn looked intrigued.

"Aren't they uncomfortable?"

"Not if it isn't tight. Keep the rear string skinny."

Valerie decided to buy her one before the prom to cheer her up. Both had to stay home with *their* boyfriends.

They sipped and watched the dwindling traffic, feeling comfortable without speaking.

Valerie thought that now was the time to raise *the* issue. "How long have you known Carl?"

"For three months. But I met him years ago."

"You look tired," Valerie said, again following David's advice to approach difficult topics indirectly.

"Lately," she agreed.

"Working too hard?"

"No more than usual."

Thinking that LeeAnn might be in the delivery room before she got an answer, Valerie asked directly.

"Have you missed a period?"

"I think that I'm pregnant."

Her calm response caused Valerie to tell herself that LeeAnn was stronger than she seemed.

"Why?"

"It's not just being tired. I'm bloated and pee a lot... and my breasts seem bigger and are sore."

"Have you tested yourself yet?"

"No."

"We'll get a kit tonight," Valerie said. "If it's 'yes' when do Carl and your parents get told?"

LeeAnn considered this. "What would you do?"

"It's different with David. We've known each other for six years. We want kids someday but not now. He couldn't survive kids, school, and working too. When's your birthday?"

"I'll be sixteen in two weeks ago. He's forty nine."

"You have a lot on him."

"Would you turn David in?"

She really loves that slimeball, Valerie thought. But why? Because he's her first boyfriend? Her self-esteem is low? God knows how her parents treated her though she and LeeAnn probably sensed that they had similar family backgrounds years ago. But David isn't thirty-three years older!

Valerie knew that attacking Carl wouldn't work: LeeAnn would just hunker down and feel more isolated.

"Whatever you need I'm with you. David too." She loved talking as if they were already married. "Do you have enough money for the abortion?"

LeeAnn's quick response surprised her.

"My father died when I was a baby. I'm having this one and it's staying with me," she said firmly.

Valerie was disappointed by her shortsightedness but understood. Until she had felt better about herself she also hungered for a child. David said that she wanted to give love to herself by identifying with a baby while loving it. Though she first felt angry and believed that he was trying to avoid commitment, she later realized he had been right.

So she determined to be LeeAnn's reliable friend. There would be plenty of others.

"When are you telling them?"

"As soon as I'm sure. Carl first. He'll help."

Valerie doubted it. He'd probably describe her as The High School Hooker.

"We better get going. The drug store closes at ten-thirty. I'll follow you."

While driving, Valerie anticipated LeeAnn's parents' reaction to her news. She didn't envy her.

CHAPTER SIX

Both stared at the wrappings of the pregnancy tests which came in varying shapes and colors.

"Which one?" LeeAnn asked.

I'm only eleven months older and she treats me like I was her big sister, Valerie thought. But, having expected this, she was prepared.

"I got a comparison off the Web. All give the same results but have different prices or come with two kits. One or two?"

"I don't know."

Now I'm her mother, Valerie thought.

"Let's get you one. The easiest to use."

"I'm not an idiot," LeeAnn pouted.

Her mother puts her down, Valerie thought. "I didn't mean that," she said soothingly. "Some have several steps or can only be used in the morning. EPT Quick Stick gives a result in two minutes, Clear Blue Easy, three. Which?" David, budding child psychiatrist, advised giving children a choice of only two.

LeeAnn chose EPT, paid for it, and they left the store.

"I'll call you."

"For sure!" Valerie insisted, hugging her. Now I've

got the sister I always wanted, she thought. Then added, and maybe daughter too.

LeeAnn drove slowly so getting home took twice as long as usual. She made sure that every traffic light turned yellow just before she reached it.

Her mother, drinking and watching *Law and Order,* waved as LeeAnn passed her bedroom to look in on her sisters. They weren't yet asleep and she tucked them in. One, barely awake, called her "mummy." Just as I related to Valerie, LeeAnn thought. I *have to* grow up and *will* make my own decisions, she vowed to herself angrily.

Once in her room, she locked the door and took the kit to the adjoining bathroom. There, sitting on the toilet seat, she read the kit's wrapper twice, as if not believing what she was doing. Then, again feeling angry for her indecision, LeeAnn ripped the carton open and carefully read the enclosed instructions, which were no different from those on the box.

She wondered where to squat and decided on the bathtub. After stripping below the waist, she peed into the yellow (an appropriate color considering her backbone, she thought) bathroom cup until it was nearly full. Then she carefully placed it on the sink and finished peeing in the toilet, now feeling more relaxed after having acted on her decision. Remembering what she had yet to do, LeeAnn again became nervous and hurriedly dried herself, deciding against washing her hands now from fear that she would tip the cup and have to wait for the results until morning.

Removing the test stick from the foil packet and holding it by the thumb grip, she dipped the absorbent tip into the urine.

Having left her watch on the night table, she counted slowly, "one, one second, two, two seconds, until reaching ten. *Twice* the time required. Then, removing the stick, she counted similarly for two minutes until the results appeared. Then she waited for another minute to be sure. And still another.

Finally she looked down and noted a pink/purple line in the small square indicating that the result would be accurate. The same was in the larger window.

She was pregnant.

LeeAnn poured the urine into the toilet and flushed it, tossed the cup in the wastebasket, then sat on the bathtub and wondered whether the child was a boy or girl. She felt it move but knew that this must be her imagination. Though believing that many adolescents would feel terrified, she felt...wonder.

Lost in fantasy, she heard a faint cry and feared it came from her child, then realized that it was her sister having another nightmare. So she put on her robe embossed with Disney characters and went to her.

One had woken the other and it took orange juice and twenty five minutes cuddling to get them back to sleep.

Then she called Valerie, who picked up on the first ring.

"Only two minutes it takes. What happened?"

"A problem with my sisters. I'm pregnant."

"Well." Valerie wasn't sure that congratulations were in order.

"Well," LeeAnn repeated.

"When are you telling them?"

"Carl's away for a month. My parents, tomorrow."

"One at a time or both?"

"Mom. When she's relaxed, on her fourth glass of wine. She'll tell dad."

"What'll they say?"

"I don't know."

"Good luck. Come to the lab for breakfast, Mother!"

Not knowing what to respond, LeeAnn grunted "ugh" and hung up.

Lying in bed, staring at the dim image of Celine Dion on the wall which was lit by the night light she always left on, LeeAnn anticipated what her parents would say. During and after their blowup and for every day thereafter.

She usually slept on her stomach but feared this would harm the baby, not knowing for sure. Valerie could find out. LeeAnn knew hardly anything about pregnancy, having first learned about sex from the school nurse to whom she ran in fright at her first period. Later, she and her mother shopped for pads. Her mother was good at buying things but never did ask what happened that day.

The more she thought, the crazier telling her parents seemed. *No way* would they let her keep the baby. If necessary, they would probably get a court order demanding she have an abortion, insisting that she was insane or retarded and both if necessary! She'd tell them after it was too late. But cooperate by letting them name the baby, smiling as she thought this.

An hour later LeeAnn thought of Ralph's probable reaction. She knew why men dated younger women. They were better looking with tighter bodies. But, likely, mostly because it made them feel younger. So being the father of an infant at forty nine should have the same effect though she doubted it and not just for a married politician. Babies meant changing diapers and being up at night, not showering together and having sex. She knew from having mothered her sisters.

So, being unsure what Ralph's reaction would be, she also wouldn't tell him until she started to show. Thankfully she was large boned so it would be awhile before even the most observant person could consider her pregnant. And Ralph might be away most months.

Now feeling comfortable with her decisions, she realized that it had been her earlier—*wrong*—analysis of the situation which kept her awake. And she decided that in the future she would pay attention to her feelings when she couldn't fall asleep or got angrier than she should about something. There *must* be a good reason and she would feel better after figuring it out. As she now did, falling asleep with the ease of the baby who she vowed to keep.

CHAPTER SEVEN

VALERIE TOOK THE Taster's Choice Instant Coffee from the cabinet before deciding on the Tetley Green Tea instead, concluding that this was healthier. She didn't know whether the tea's antioxidants could benefit a fetus but knew that LeeAnn needed all the help she could possibly get.

Valerie felt angry after learning of LeeAnn's pregnancy. Only recently did her life feel settled and her present involvement with LeeAnn's crisis disturbed this and made her jealous. She hadn't wanted to have her abortion two years earlier but was sure that having a baby then would have wrecked her relationship with David—particularly since he wasn't the father.

It happened when he was heavily into his studies. Feeling neglected and wanting to make him jealous, she had sex with a boy a year older than herself. Thankfully, David never found out and she was ashamed of how dumb she had behaved.

Now, being unable to imagine life without him, she silently vowed fidelity and that they would have a good marriage. One which was very different from that of her parents, who couldn't live together or separate and so drove their kids crazy.

Her older brother started sniffing glue at eight, progressing (?) to beer at thirteen. "He's trying to make himself feel better, David said. Which she told him that she already knew. Then he apologized, saying that doctors behaved grandiosely to help them better cope with their sometimes unbearable feelings. Those *she* once had and he had ignored.

Her thinking returned to how to talk LeeAnn out of having the baby even though she knew that most pregnant girls could recite arguments against teenage motherhood. But Valerie would try, subtly. Or had planned to until LeeAnn walked through the door, glowing. Valerie felt angry again.

"Sit down...mother...'fore you fall," Valerie said, speaking the "m" word softly so that only LeeAnn could hear. Even if no one was around it was best not to take any chances.

"Tea?" Valerie asked.

"And yogurt."

"Almost ready."

"Two sugars."

They began eating.

"Yep," LeeAnn said.

"Is that mother speak?"

"I should be scared but I'm not."

"You will be when you tell your mother."

LeeAnn became silent. Suddenly, Valerie wished that LeeAnn had confided in someone else.

"I'm waiting for awhile."

"For how long?"

"Until it's too late for an abortion."

"Why?"

"Why what?"

Now I understand why mothers murder their children, Valerie thought. Then, as she forced herself to be calm, a thought popped into her mind: it might her been her. *If* David had not insisted on the abortion and she needed him more than anything. Maybe she was angry because LeeAnn possessed a strength which she hadn't.

"Why have the child?"

"I want to."

"It's no fun being a mother."

"I'm mothering my sisters."

As if to say, what do you know about being a parent? She's right, Valerie thought, I'm putting her down like David does to me. "When will you tell?"

"During the sixth month to my parents. Carl, when I show."

"Do you know how far along you are?"

"I missed two periods."

"So, in four months. How can I help?"

Now LeeAnn became tearful.

"I *am* scared. I don't know what to do or have anyone."

"Except me." Valerie felt hooked but she also felt glad to be involved. Maybe nature makes women dumb about having babies, she thought, why else would they go through it?

"Can I tell David? He can help."

"Does he blabber?"

"Barely to me."

"OK. But just to him."

"I don't know anything either," Valerie said, though this wasn't true. She had spent days reading about pregnancy before her abortion. "I'll get stuff off the Web. Eating right and keeping calm is important. We can't meet here. It's too public. We'll meet at your house to do homework. Your mom can't object to that."

Both smiled and Valerie wondered what David would say when he learned.

CHAPTER EIGHT

THE HOUSE WAS huge, Valerie thought. More a mansion than part of a suburban development—on minimum six acre lots. She had read that a nearby smaller house sold for three million plus and wondered why LeeAnn's parents didn't hire a nanny to care for the twins who kept interrupting them. Though she hoped that the annoyance would convince LeeAnn to do what Valerie considered best. Until LeeAnn's comment which was expressed while she lay on the floor with her legs raised, a position she had read was healthy for pregnant women.

"I feel *so* happy," LeeAnn said.

Valerie started feeling depressed again. Until she remembered her role in this Scarsdale soap opera.

"Mothers-to-be should."

The Monsters chose this moment to wander into the room and snuggle next to LeeAnn. Not even a TV serial would have such a bizarre scene, Valerie thought. Alcoholic mother downstairs, teenage daughter pregnant by an old slime ball upstairs, devoted friend helping. Only incest was missing. The world was really crazy.

Both stared at The Monsters. There could be no talking with them around.

"We make sundaes as soon as I finish my homework," LeeAnn told them softly.

"You're not doing homework," one said. "Not doing anything," the other chimed in. The teens ignored them. Finally, sensing that they wouldn't get any attention, the children left the room though having the last word.

"Babies lay on the floor."

LeeAnn stuck out her tongue and Valerie started to before reminding herself that one person had to behave like an adult in this house.

With the door again closed, LeeAnn asked, "what should I do first?"

Valerie tried to remember what she had read. She left the bed and sat cross-legged beside LeeAnn on the floor. "You don't have to do anything new. But everything happening to you effects the baby. If you don't get good food neither will they. The same with getting upset. Do you take vitamins?"

"What're they?" LeeAnn asked with a grin.

"You are now. Calcium/magnesium/zinc—the six large white ones. Two multi-vitamins—the red ones. Three vitamin C's—the small white ones. One vitamin E—yellow. All taken daily." Valerie tossed her a large Ziploc bag containing four opaque bottles with labeled instructions on each .

"What if I won't?" LeeAnn asked, though Valerie noted that she had listened carefully. She would follow the instructions.

"Your baby is deformed." Stronger words than she had intended and LeeAnn became tearful.

"Never! Whatever you say."

"What *we* decide is best," Valerie corrected her.

A knock on the door ended their conversation.

"Mom."

"In," LeeAnn called. They don't waste words here, Valerie thought. Adding or food, as she noticed the mother's figure.

LeeAnn's mother looked stunning but discordant for forty-one. Her hair was glossy black though too long. With too full lips and Valerie wondered if she used injectable collagen or the newer allergy free Hylaform Gel which she had believed was available only in Europe. Small, firm breasts pressed against her tight black shirt, this color being accented by the white polish on her short square fingernails and the shiny cherry red polish on her toes. Her lipstick was light Apricot and her eye shadow was subtle. Like her Hermes perfume, 24 Faubourg. Whatever LeeAnn believed, Valerie would bet that her mother wore thongs beneath her tight unbelted jeans.

She gazed with alcoholic euphoria. "Come over often," she said to Valerie. "LeeAnn's too serious and it's good for her to have a friend. To be a real teen involved with her prom and things like that. Soon she'll be at college. Then have a mother's never ending workdays. I'll see to my little ones now."

LeeAnn's mother left as quickly as she had entered, leaving a faint scent and amused looks on the faces of the teens.

"Mom," LeeAnn said.

"Is *that* what you want to be?" Valerie joked.

LeeAnn responded with seething anger.

"I'll *never* be like her!" she burst out.

Valerie told the last information she remembered.

"No exercise except swimming. Definitely no bike riding or jogging till the baby's born. Get it?"

"How about sex?"

"I thought Carl was away."

"He'll be back next month."

"It's OK now but ask me again in your seventh month."

"I can always help him," LeeAnn said.

Out a tenth floor window, Valerie thought, as they began their Honors math homework. An hour later LeeAnn got up, touched her stomach in a protective way, then went to give her sisters the sundaes she had promised. Valerie was curious what a three million dollar house looked like and accompanied her.

The house was like any other house but bigger. Downstairs was a hallway off which was a living room. There was also a kitchen and dining room, library, and entrances to the basement and a four car garage. Upstairs were seven bedrooms with attached bathrooms. The parents' bedroom was farthest down the hall, being separated from the children's by unused ones.

Valerie was impressed at how quiet the house was for the soundproofing was much better than in her house. Everything was.

Each room had a fireplace with logs stacked and ready for lighting. The downstairs doors were paneled with heavy brass fixtures and gold painted molding, except for the one to the basement which was stained glass.

The living room was made to look even larger by its mirrored panels, and was divided into separate areas by sofa and chair arrangements. It was decorated in a monochrome scheme with the hard black furniture being softened by the cream colored carpet and walls. Lighting was indirect and needed for the windows were small. Their sculptured security bars gave the otherwise elegant room the sense of a fortress.

The kitchen had a beamed ceiling, hardwood floor, wooden cabinets, and commercial sized refrigerator and stove. Despite the friendly strawberry print curtains, the room only *seemed* as if it were used by a bustling family.

But the children's' rooms were definitely lived in. Traditional furniture of natural wood complemented painted wicker baskets filled with stuffed animals and toys. Though the fifty two inch projection TVs gave the rooms a garish un-childlike atmosphere. Like the HBO movie the children were watching which LeeAnn quickly turned off.

"No and I mean it! *No* movie watching unless I'm with you. You don't deserve sundaes," LeeAnn stormed at her sisters.

To end their tantrums, Valerie asked the girls, "What was it about?"

"Two gay guys," said one. Her twin corrected her, "One was bi and really wanted his lover's sister."

Valerie shut up. Though ignorant about babies, LeeAnn obviously knew how to be a mother.

Valerie tried to help. "I'm hungry."

"You're getting sundaes only 'cause Val wants one. It'll be the last until your birthday."

The children immediately calmed down as if trusting that LeeAnn didn't mean what she said. Despite their age both wanted to be carried. To Valerie's surprise, LeeAnn readily agreed.

Each teen carried a child to a room at their end of the hallway. The room was sixteen by eighteen feet and held a microwave, blender, toaster oven, smaller refrigerator than downstairs, sink/garbage disposal, dishwasher, cabinets with children's unbreakable glassware, and counter with stools.

The refrigerator held ice cream, yogurt, milk, juice, Gouda and Jarlsberg cheeses, butter, mayonnaise, strawberry, pineapple, and peach preserves, and English muffins and crackers. Cabinets were stocked with canned tuna and salmon, and chocolate chip cookies and raisins in orange capped plastic containers. A small locked cabinet held aspirin substitute and first-aid supplies. Affixed to the wall by the phone were medical instructions and the numbers of police and fire departments, pediatrician and emergency room. Valerie was impressed.

"Who set this up?"

"I did," LeeAnn responded.

Thinking that she might be underestimating her friend, Valerie again tried to change LeeAnn's mind.

"Did you date much before Carl?"

"Two."

"Boyfriends?"

"Times."

Then Valerie again followed David's advice: it's easier to get someone thinking if you tell them a story.

"I had only one boyfriend before David—for just two weeks. I wonder if I'll regret it years from now. Maybe want leave him with the kids and get an apartment and motorcycle and boyfriend and do what I never did."

LeeAnn watched her sisters eat. Valerie was about to try again when LeeAnn nodded towards them. "Later."

Which was after the children were in bed.

"I love him," LeeAnn said.

"Does he love you?"

"How can you know for sure?"

"You can't...for sure."

"I care about him. And trust him enough to tell him everything." But not that you're pregnant, Valerie thought.

"Do you think you'll marry him someday?"

"Possibly...probably. *After* his divorce. Now that he's away I feel I need to have him around. I guess that's love."

Could be sex too, Valerie thought, abandoning this attempt. Soon enough LeeAnn would see him as he is. But maybe not—some women manage to stay dumb about love all their lives.

"I better get going."

"What if I need you? You can have a room down the hall."

So Valerie stayed. She loved the house and liked having a sister, even one who behaved like an idiot.

Both girls were tired. After borrowing underwear for the next day, Valerie went to her room and put on the pajamas emblazoned with Disney characters which all children in this house wore regardless of age.

The night table was locked. Valerie was curious what lay within and her search soon succeeded in finding the spare key taped to its underside. Within was a manila envelope containing an eight by ten inch photo of LeeAnn's mother. Naked, and signed, "For Ralph, my only love."

Valerie was surprised, having believed that only teenagers shaved their pubic hair. Beneath this photo was a formal picture of a good looking man in his forties, dressed in a suit and tie. His photo was definitely more cautious and for good reason: LeeAnn's father was named Walter.

Before falling asleep, Valerie wondered how much LeeAnn knew about her mother's life.

CHAPTER NINE

THE MEN RELAXED at the end of a long day. One was seated behind the large desk on which his feet lay as the other sprawled on a sofa.

"You live dangerously," the elderly assistant said.

This would have been an unhealthy comment for most employees but the man had known Ralph since childhood. He even baby sat him during an emergency while his father narrowly avoided indictment. Trust derives from personal experience and William Tower, Esq. had been trusted by both the father and his son. Not for legal advice deriving from the Harvard training which he barely remembered. But for his ability to offer solutions so simple and effective that many troubled government officials termed him "The Lord." And also for his warm relationships with reporters. These made him well worth the $147,000 salary he could easily multiply elsewhere. He stayed at his job because of his promise to Ralph's dying father that he would try to guide his son's life, even if the son was far more impulsive than his father ever had been.

Tower's loyalty was similar to that of ancient butlers in English households. This made understandable why the only TV program he watched, repeatedly, was the taped series, *Upstairs/Downstairs,* which described the fictionalized daily life of an Edwardian household as viewed by family and servants. But he viewed the pre-World War One episodes only, for he disliked the rapid changes in the later ones. His best friend, also a bachelor, was a justice of the United States Supreme Court. Both were solitary men.

Long before, Tower had adopted Ralph's family as his own, regarding its members critically but with understanding. And sometimes he thought, with love.

"I never date a woman whose ex-husband carries a gun," Ralph joked, responding to Tower's assertion that he lived dangerously. Ralph didn't like to think about his behavior.

"The present woman doesn't need one."

"That's over."

"For you or both?"

"Isn't it the same?"

"Which is why you don't date a woman whose ex carries a gun," Tower said.

Though Ralph was approaching fifty, Tower still found that counseling him indirectly worked best. For forty years he had planted his seeds of advice; slowly, very slowly, some had ripened.

But this wasn't an evening for criticism for that day Ralph, United States Senator Ralph Beekman, had achieved his long sought goal of appointment to the Oversight Subcommittee on American Intelligence Activity. He wanted this since entering the senate seven years earlier though Tower wondered why: Appropriations,

Banking, even the Judiciary committee were far more useful. Perhaps, he thought, it was the attraction which covert activities have for bullying personalities.

But, being both father figure *and* employee, Tower fulfilled Ralph's desire, as he always did.

A distrusting senator had stood in the way. Just before takeoff and flying drunk as usual, he had bumped another passenger as both sought the bathroom. A near scuffle ensued and the senator insisted that the man be removed from the plane, describing him as "a drunk and a menace." This was done. Next day the man sued the airline for twenty million dollars.

It appealed to the senator who immediately apologized to the man, took him to dinner, then sent a case of champagne and two of his state's best bourbon. When a reporter lauded his generosity the senator responded, "The restaurant owner's a friend, a distiller donated the whiskey and importer the champagne. All I did was to phone and apologize."

But the public never learned this statement. Tower quickly spoke to the reporter who thereafter printed another remark which Tower suggested: "I apologized to the man because it's a fine thing to apologize to an individual. But I'd never apologize to a mob. The first is gracious; the second cowardly." This statement was nationally applauded as reflecting the consummate wisdom of an elder statesman—and Ralph got his appointment.

Yet Tower wondered if always helping him was wise. He had gotten him out of the usual scrapes which middle-aged men have when confronting their mortality. And Ralph *did* mature. Now he no longer told off-color jokes and drank less in public. But he still enjoyed engaging in risky behavior, like with LeeAnn.

Ralph thought he was being secretive but Tower paid all his expenses, including that of the New York apartment doorman's Christmas gift. One from Ralph; a far larger present from him. First bedding the mother and then the daughter. The man had no decency, Tower thought, though he smiled like the indulgent father he had become.

He wondered again whether to raise this matter but decided that it wasn't timely. It would be better to wait until he was desperate, like with his wife threatening a publicized divorce unless the affairs ended.

Ralph complained that Tower was overly protective but this wasn't true. Tower knew his place. And Ralph *was* a United States senator, though one who behaved more recklessly than most.

"I'm getting old," Ralph said.

Tower nodded from the sofa, sensing that more was coming. Except for his seating position, he resembled a psychoanalyst awaiting a pregnant comment from their patient.

"I have to think beyond the senate."

Now Tower knew. Ralph's desire for the ultimate goal of many politicians who rise beyond their state legislature. Gerald Ford had escaped it though becoming president. Tower wondered why he thought of Ford now for Beekman and he were so different, Ford being the most honorable man he had ever known.

And far from the blockhead he was described by reporters who misread his lack of guile. Ford *took* his advice. Particularly after Ford had commented that "if Lincoln were alive today he'd be turning over in his grave." He then pleaded to be saved from future gaffes. Which Tower enjoyed doing for he considered Gerald Ford and his wife to be emblematic of the finest American characteristics.

Tower had first met them fifty years before: a Midwestern couple who might have stepped from a Norman Rockwell painting. Tower was visiting Washington with his family and, when asked what he expected to be doing in five years, spontaneously blurted "attend Harvard Law School." All except Ford smiled.

Ford had graduated in the upper third of his famous nineteen forty one Yale Law class which produced notable political successes and a current Supreme Court justice. But many thought him foolish and Tower again considered why. Perhaps because he was so unpretentious. Buying food, washing dishes. Above all: living an honest life.

During senate hearings before his nomination for vice president, Tower asked how he managed to stay so pure a politician that the four hundred fifty FBI agents investigating found nothing questionable in his background. Ford gave one of his broad smiles and then said that he was taught how to live by his parents: "you darn well better tell the truth and live an honest life if you don't want to pay a penalty down the road."

Tower wondered if Ralph even knew what the truth was—and forget about honesty. But he consistently attracted voters by paying attention to local issues. And despite lacking seniority his name was associated with so many public projects that neither had found amusing the naive question of a child as to whether he was a builder. To which Ralph smiled and gave one of his best lines: "I build America." This, in only his fourth year in the senate, which indicated that his goal was the presidency even then.

"When?" Tower asked.

"Next year. Five years is too long to wait. What do you think?"

Tower didn't like thinking of him as president but knew that the country had survived worse. And better. FDR lied to and manipulated everyone, and had feared Huey Long's effect on the 1936 election until his opportune assassination which rumor held...but Roosevelt never had an affair with mother *and* daughter.

Still, whatever Tower believed, Ralph wouldn't listen. Few who came down with the presidential addiction stopped until they struck out.

"It takes a manager," Tower said.

"There's none better than you."

So Tower accepted this job too, as both knew that he would. Then he planted another seed of advice.

"Well before your time, an attorney from my state ran for Congress. In order to win he needed the support of an elderly newspaper editor. They spoke and spoke and the editor finally said, 'I can tell you're a good person and we'll probably endorse you. But before I do I just want to make sure that you're not one of those damned lawyers.' The man gulped, then said, 'Yes sir I am. But I've never been any good at it.'"

Ralph smashed his fist on the desk, rattling the heavy phone.

"That's exactly why I need you for my campaign," he said. "You know what's important is winning and not how."

Tower smiled. His seed suggesting candor had obviously not yet germinated. He sat thinking in his office long after Ralph left.

He was lucky to have learned about LeeAnn. And luckier still if he were able to thwart public knowledge of the affair, for a presidential candidacy meant hordes of reporters. Tower now needed continuous information. This could be gotten in the one way that both had joked about—and would cause Ralph to fire even him were it to be discovered. Tower must have him watched.

So, like the parent who reads their teenager's mail, hoping not to be found out but having a prepared excuse if they are, Tower was ready. His actions would be described as having been assertively protective: wanting plausible explanations ready before embarrassing activities might become public. The recording bugs would be described, by *Tower's* employee, as high frequency scrambler devices meant to circumvent recorders.

Tower distrusted investigative agencies for reputable ones usually refused this type of work, He leaned towards hiring an individual. One close to his age and so less likely to have a private agenda. A retired intelligence officer? But he would have to be quick thinking and technically competent. Then he remembered a funny story from someone he hadn't spoken with in fifteen years.

The officer was asked by a black congressman to stop describing covert activities as "black" since he couldn't figure out how to explain to his constituents why he consistently voted against appropriations for "operations in the black world." The room rocked with laughter though all recognized the validity of his request. The officer changed the adjective to "special access" though the Pentagon, informally, still called them "black."

He also had good technical capabilities and once demonstrated an Electronic Countermeasures Receiver which didn't deactivate "bugs" but located them, enabling one to listen in by becoming a pirate receiver and "bugging the bugger."

After retiring from the military he worked for a think tank in California until his wife died, then retired to a house in Stone Ridge, New York, thirty miles north of West Point. Well before the town became a weekend home for New York City models and media people, and Tower wondered how he fit in.

He picked up the phone to dial information, then decided it would be best to call from a pay phone which he did that night. The two chatted about old times and Tower got himself invited to Stone Ridge, to discuss "a confidential proposal of some importance."

CHAPTER TEN

LEEANN WAS BEING insufferable. So content and sure even without knowing her parents' reaction. Maybe pregnancy did that, Valerie thought, and felt jealous again. Then, imagining her future life with David and viewing LeeAnn's pregnancy as *her* trial run, she became LeeAnn's friend. Again.

LeeAnn was in her fourth month and looked healthier. She reliably took the vitamins which Valerie advised. They were together so much that LeeAnn's mother asked Valerie to call her by her first name, Elizabeth (not Liz as in Lizzie Borden, LeeAnn added under her breath).

LeeAnn did all the cooking at home and followed David's relayed suggestions about healthy eating. The Monsters didn't object to the changes and their parents didn't notice, food being secondary to alcohol in their lives.

Some of David's recommendations were unusual. Being interested in herbal medicine, he gave Valerie raspberry leaf for LeeAnn's tea. She was to drink this beginning in her eighteenth week, three cups a day mixed with orange juice, saying that it helped to regulate the uterine muscle. And Viburnum prunifolium, four milliliters three times a day during her last two months.

Valerie wondered if David had a thing for pregnant women. Particularly after his joke that when helping deliver babies he tended to get his fingers in the wrong place.

The girls were in LeeAnn's room. LeeAnn's feet were upraised and Valerie sprawled nearby. The Monsters were pigging out on gigantic sundaes. Watching cartoons, they claimed.

"Carl's returning next week," LeeAnn sighed. Valerie wondered if being pregnant made women Victorian. It didn't with her but she was never this far along.

"What did he say?"

"Mom talked to him."

"When are you seeing him?"

"I'll call him..."

"Which is why I wanted you over," Valerie finished her sentence.

"I'm not nervous. Just...expectant."

"Like being pregnant?"

A month before Valerie would have gotten a pillow in the face. Now LeeAnn sighed again. "How would you tell him?"

"Sit down daddy."

"Seriously."

"For serious, I don't know." She couldn't imagine how she would have told David that her baby wasn't his. But Valerie felt that some suggestion was in order.

"The baby comes from your loving. Wait till then."

"Do I show?"

"Will it matter to him?"

Moments passed.

"I should have an exam. Can David do it?"

"David's *not* doing it. He's not in practice." Or getting his fingers inside you she wanted to add.

"Who then?"

Now it's my problem, Valerie thought. But not a big one.

"Planned Parenthood in New York. They're cheap, and you'll use another name."

"Clinton," LeeAnn responded impishly.

"Whatever," Valerie said, feeling depressed again.

"You'll come?"

"Of course."

Valerie called information for the number and LeeAnn scheduled an appointment for "Hillary Gore" at six the next day. She was told to bring one hundred and fifty five dollars. Cash.

"There goes my prom dress," LeeAnn said.

"You won't fit. The name's cute."

Valerie slept over. LeeAnn had asked her to and Valerie loved staying in a rich person's house. Good thing I'm marrying a doctor, she thought, but then hated herself for thinking it.

The photos were still there: shaved pubis and distinguished looking man. Valerie wondered who he was and whether the condoms behind the books belonged to

LeeAnn or to her mother. Mysterious love piled on mysterious love, but tacky not glamorous.

After carefully replacing the condoms where she found them, five left from a box of twelve, she got into bed leaving a small light on. She wasn't as fearless as others thought. Only David knew about her nightmares and he couldn't figure them out though having another in this house would be appropriate considering the atmosphere.

Worry about their math exam overshadowed other concerns as the girls drove to New York City in LeeAnn's Mercedes SUV. A sweet sixteen gift from her father. Really just a station wagon, she said, but Valerie would change fathers any day. Her's had wandering hands until she slugged him.

The Planned Parenthood exam held no surprise. Two blood samples were taken and a urine sample collected. Then tests for diabetes, toxemia, hereditary diseases, German measles, and how well she was producing red blood cells. Her abdomen was measured, vagina and cervix examined, and smears were taken for Pap and gonorrhea tests. Instruction in diet and exercise followed and LeeAnn smiled at Valerie who felt pleased that her advice had been correct.

"Will the father be the birth partner?" the nurse asked. She didn't look much older than them and Valerie wondered how much she knew.

"He's a Marine in Germany. I haven't told him yet. We'll get married over his next leave," Hillary/LeeAnn replied in an earnest, worried tone. Like she had just left her Scarsdale cotton mill town for the first time that day, working there as a pin-girl in an antiquated non-automated bowling alley. Maybe she didn't even know *how* she got pregnant. The nurse's eyes widened.

"I'm sure you will Ms. Gore, but he'll be away a lot. Can your friend be the birth partner?"

Both stared at her and Valerie agreed. LeeAnn had no one else, and the baby's father would soon be accusing her of rape before her parents tried to strangle her.

"Some of our best partners are friends," the nurse said reassuringly. Adding, "men can have problems with feelings."

"Have you given birth yet?" the nurse asked Valerie.

She must think that Scarsdale is the East Coast's Appalachia, Valerie thought, but said sweetly, "My husband is in the same unit. We're waiting until we're married...and in base housing."

"Yeas," the nurse said, wanting to defend her patient but not to alienate either girl. She opened her mouth twice without saying anything. Then she handed them booklets describing stress reduction and massage techniques, and enrolled them in weekly classes "with other teens like you." Valerie wondered how many of them came in a Mercedes SUV with disability and working press parking permits provided by their father.

While driving home they smiled at each other.

"So when you telling Carl?" Valerie asked.

"He's back for his twentieth wedding anniversary tonight. Maybe Friday in New York. I'm at your house all weekend if anyone asks."

"Who would? Your Planned Parenthood nurse? Hope y'all don't meet. What about The Monsters?"

LeeAnn was silent.

"No," Valerie said firmly.

"Well I *can't* leave them home or take them. They love the City and David's apartment is downtown. You can see how he is with kids. The ones besides you," LeeAnn added with a smile. Then stuck her tongue out.

Valerie agreed. Partly because the car swerved whenever LeeAnn was upset so it was likely that they wouldn't survive if Valerie didn't agree. Also because she did wonder how David would relate to children. First she experiences a virtual pregnancy and now a virtual family.

They gossiped the usual, who was sleeping with who, until this topic petered out for both now felt too old. Their long silence was ended by a gasp from Valerie after they entered LeeAnn's house and passed the open library door. There, seated facing her mother on the sofa, was a tall man dressed in a black suit and red/black regimental tie. The one in the photo.

"Come in LeeAnn," Elizabeth gushed, "Ralph is waiting for your father."

CHAPTER ELEVEN

TOWER ASSUMED THAT there was some psychological reason why he never learned how to drive since he was the only youth growing up in his small Missouri town who didn't. But therapy wasn't for him although his life and New York state politics would be easier if Ralph were so inclined. Then Tower wouldn't have to be making this one hundred and sixty dollar taxi ride from New York City. The first two taxi drivers asked what state Stone Ridge was in and telling them that it was due north of West Point didn't help. The third, from India, knew where it was for his brother owned a restaurant in Ellenville which was west of Stone Ridge on Route 209.

So he settled into the cab, already feeling uneasy because of his inability to find the seat belt. He didn't like cars or flying but knew the Washington subway system better than most.

To discourage chatter, Tower ostentatiously opened his briefcase and removed and studied a blank legal pad. The driver stopped talking and, while waiting at a light, put on headphones to listen to a Dean Koontz thriller, *Dark Rivers Of The Heart*. Noting the title, *Tower* felt that it well described the source of his mission.

Beekman's behavior was puzzling. Tower had never married and long envied the good fortune of those who did. He wondered why Beekman jeopardized his settled family life, even if it wasn't as perfect as it appeared.

The Beekman family fortune originated with taxis which delivered liquor during prohibition. Later came marriages to Wall Street partners and a chemical industry CEO. One daughter did marry a college teacher, but one who worked at Oak Ridge and advised American presidents on defense matters.

Ralph was the family's political hope. Why Ralph's father developed this desire he couldn't imagine. But maybe because there was nothing else for him to do but to watch his fortune, which was now in the nine figure range, be increased by hired managers.

Sports or philanthropy never interested him. Power did, and he groomed his son for political office since his childhood. Ralph followed his father's wishes and his father never opposed his.

Ralph first became a father at sixteen or, as his third stepmother put it, she became a grandmother before she gave birth. His father procreated until his late seventies, this giving Ralph enough brothers, sisters, half-brothers, half-sisters, ex-step-mothers and other combinations to make Tower dizzy. Unconcerned with fact, Ralph called them cousin, brother, sister, mom or by name depending on how he felt. Their sexual interest he always got right.

Ralph liked young women and, recently, younger ones too. When Tower raised the issue, being concerned with risk and not morality for even the notorious JFK hadn't been that foolish, he got the adolescent answer he expected.

"All over seventeen and the age of consent. They'll never gossip. They love me."

Tower agreed, but feared their parents' reaction. Though possibly it would be just admiration for Ralph was influential and it was a different world than when Tower grew up. And not a better one in some ways, he concluded.

But LeeAnn had been fifteen when their affair began and he hoped that Ralph wouldn't get more scandalous. Then he'd quit despite his debt to Ralph's father who had paid for Tower's education and saved his accountant/father from jail when, fearing the loss of his job, he concealed high-level embezzlement by his boss.

But Tower would stay as long as he could: retirement wasn't for him and where else could a sixty nine year old who had worked at one job for all of his life feel comfortable?

As the taxi arrived he wondered how much to tell. The money would be attractive (three hundred fifty dollars a day plus unaudited expenses) but he knew this alone wouldn't matter to one with two pensions, a mortgage-free home and, soon, Social Security. Tower had checked this. But boredom might be weighing heavily on him.

He paid the driver and, while walking towards the door, couldn't remember his friend's name. He had started forgetting such details. But he was still able to care for himself and hadn't yet left his home wearing one shoe or gotten lost while traveling a familiar route, these being symptoms which his doctor advised him to watch for. His mother had died of Alzheimer Disease and he hoped for a more dignified end.

"Let me take that," his friend said, reaching for the suitcase.

"I'm not that much older than you," was the smiling response as he ignored the outstretched hand.

During gossip about Stone Ridge and their tour of the garden, Tower remembered his friend's name: Paul Dalling.

"Fifteen years since we spoke. The older I get the faster time goes. When you're young you think you have all the time in the world..."

"And when you're older," Tower interrupted, "you realize only that can't be changed."

They drank a local Merlot, Tower more than usual. He was nervous for this was only the second time in his career that he had behaved independently of Beekman family instructions. And having one's boss shadowed was the ultimate in self-assertion. Self-protection too? A man bedding an adolescent might be doing even more criminal acts, and inviting prosecutors who knew that no fortune was gained wholly innocently, or maintained without offshore accounts free from prying eyes. Though this was now less frequent since a Grand Cayman banker cut a deal from an American jail by providing computer records of his clients' transactions.

Tower's intended yarn seemed shopworn the more he considered it. Dalling had heard every lie.

"What's this confidential matter—government work?" he asked, refilling his guest's glass. Not facing Tower but listening closely.

"Beekman."

"Even the *National Inquirer* doesn't bother about him anymore."

"But if he runs for president..."

"You could wind up as Attorney General. He might well choose worse. Would you accept?"

Tower waved a deprecating hand. "I'm soon for a rocking chair. You?"

Dalling gazed at his garden. The youngest of his four children was gone, attending college in New Paltz with her boyfriend and their child. It was a new age and uncomfortable, like Beekman's current behavior.

"Retirement isn't for either of us. And you always hated to travel," Dalling responded.

The truth is best, the elder Beekman once advised, after trying everything else first. But now Tower began with it.

"I'm organizing his presidential campaign."

"Are you here as his manager?"

"No. I need your help and I never was here."

Dalling remembered similar words being spoken by officials who lied during later investigations and he had no intention of exhausting his savings on lawyers. The silence lengthened.

"It's not like that," Tower said, sensing Dalling's dwindling interest. "Only private funds are being used. I want him watched and recordings made in the City apartment he uses. *My* apartment. I want to know *first* what reporters can discover."

"Is it risky?" Dalling would make his own assessment.

"No."

Dalling's eyes returned to his garden.

"Minimal," Tower corrected. "You'll have his weekly schedule. The phone is mine too and nothing will be made public. I want to know who he dates and their ages. They've been too young lately."

"Another adolescent mid-lifer. Don't trust anyone under sixty."

"Three hundred fifty a day plus expenses until he's elected or drops out of the race. Everything to be destroyed after I hear it. Two hundred thousand bonus on election day. Win or lose, you win."

"Why should I do it?"

"Because you're smart and, as you say, retirement isn't for us. You have a beautiful garden but your country needs you."

"Does it need him? They say he identifies so completely with America that he thinks he owns it."

"A little grandiose but he gets things done."

"Including a bridge named after you if you die prematurely."

Both smiled and Tower sensed that he would take the job. Dalling's life had lacked meaning since his wife's death. He would feel good having a daily goal besides traveling to the supermarket.

"How will I be paid?"

"Cash every two weeks. Just two friends talking over old times over a cozy fire."

"What's the contingency plan if things blow up?"

"You're doing research for his election committee. Put together a thousand pages on defense issues. If anything drops, I'll lead the investigation and you'll be consultant to it. I chose you because only someone with your experience could find out the truth."

"I'll take monthly checks. It's more businesslike and I do pay my taxes. No other contact between us. My wife's gardening business had a voice mail. (He handed Tower a card from his wallet.) In an emergency call from a pay phone. I'll be paged in seconds. What should we call you?"

A word popped into Tower's mind.

"Call me *worried*," he said.

CHAPTER TWELVE

ELIZABETH HAD THE relaxed look which her seventh glass of wine of the day usually produced. Although twenty five years older, she could almost pass as LeeAnn's sister and Valerie remembered David's comment that some alcoholics retained their youthful appearance even as their insides rotted away. Still, the scene looked enviable: mother and her confidante, daughter and her friend, all sharing experiences before a bay window shaded by a tall maple. As improbable an event as those in the classic movies which Valerie loved.

"*Finally* home," Elizabeth gushed, "you'll want milk and cookies." Valerie wondered if she would offer to explain menstruation next. Or remembered where the refrigerator was. In her condition she wouldn't trust her to carry a tray.

"Thanks mom, but we pigged out," LeeAnn answered, also not wanting her walking.

Silence.

Thankfully, The Monsters' screams then reverberated through the house. They were following LeeAnn's orders never to go downstairs after bedtime unless it was an emergency or there would be one when she saw them.

"The girls'll work it out," Elizabeth observed sweetly, as they took this opportunity to leave the room. Which LeeAnn did. Changing her sister's sheets took less time than getting them back to sleep. One whispered to Valerie that her sister got scared because of what they saw on the *Playboy* channel. Valerie quickly changed the subject, not wanting LeeAnn to get upset. "It's important for pregnant woman to stay calm," David had advised. When the crisis was over and they were again alone, LeeAnn asked, "How do you like Ralph?"

"Good looking...he resembles the older Clark Gable."

"Gable?"

"A movie star from before your time."

"He's good in bed too."

LeeAnn smiled impishly like she finally let the cat out from the bag. Valerie considered it the leopard from its cage. LeeAnn was a total idiot in a loony family. Valerie thought that she must have been crazy getting involved with them.

Pushing Carl/Ralph from a window was too charitable: he should be dropped into a pool of piranha wearing cement shoes. And if LeeAnn knew the truth about he and her mother, Valerie was confident that she would mix the concrete. Keep her calm, David had urged. So Valerie changed the subject a little.

"Why lie to me about his name?"

"People talk."

"But I'm your *friend*!"

"And my first real one who's teaching me how to be one."

Valerie felt touched and her anger was replaced by her silent renewed vow to help LeeAnn.

"Do you have sex here?" Valerie asked.

"Never. The Monsters see everything."

So the condoms weren't hers, Valerie thought, and wondered how much the children did know. She hoped for everyone's sake that LeeAnn's mother wasn't kindergarten gossip.

"He looks familiar."

"You don't watch the news."

"Our TV screen hit a beer can and my dad never trusted one again."

"He's *Senator* Ralph. But that's not why I'm involved with him," LeeAnn added. "He's gentle and caring and really listens though my parents would never understand."

I can't imagine why, Valerie thought. A United States senator who seduces a mother and her teenage daughter. She wondered how young he went. Could this explain why The Monsters were so precocious about sex?

Sometimes you don't see the things closest to you, David had said. If all survived she would get them to a church. Anyone. Maybe the late minister/author's Norman Vincent Peale's Marble Collegiate for some of his *Power of Positive Thinking*.

LeeAnn blabbed on about Ralph's virtues until Valerie said that she was tired and went to her room.

When she was alone, she threw herself onto the bed and cried at the unfairness for all who have to endure inept parents. Then she became calmer and investigated the desk drawer again. Elizabeth's photo was gone but Ralph's was still there, atop the draft of a letter.

The handwriting, on lined school book sheets, was elegant, even with some words being scratched out and others substituted. Addressed to "Dearest Ralph" it read:

"I've considered what you said and agree. One must behave as they sense is best at the apparent moment for success. Which will occur if it's meant to. I believe that one's destiny is achieved through determination and hard work.

"Among your great gifts is the ability to see people as they can be and helping them to realize their potential. But you don't recognize how unusual this talent is.

"You can see from my photo that I've done as you asked. Do you love it? I hope so.

"You'll always be my priority although I realize that this nation, which you'll soon lead, must be yours. However I can help, in whatever you ask, without question, always..."

Stunned, Valerie replaced the letter and re-locked the drawer. Both mother and daughter really loved that creep.

She wondered how many other women did. *Could tens of millions of voters be attracted to him? Women and men?* For the first time in her life Valerie felt helpless.

While in grade school she had encouraged the protest of other students who hated their principal and believed this was instrumental in his firing. But a senator. They had power and money. She had...David, maybe. Until he learned everything. And possibly The Monsters. The odds weren't good: a teenage idiot and two five year olds against one of the richest men in America.

Lying under the covers, Valerie thought about her last night together with David. Wanting him inside of her, she fondled herself and became moist. A few minutes later, as relaxed as she could be without having him lie next to her, her anxiety disappeared in the grandiosity and exuberance of adolescence. The odds might be huge but she felt confident. Though she still planned to check out Marble Collegiate Church.

CHAPTER THIRTEEN

VALERIE WAS NERVOUS. She felt even more troubled as the date for The Monsters' sleep-over arrived and she realized that she would be *their mother* all weekend. David had readily accepted her need to do a favor for LeeAnn. But Valerie didn't tell him the whole story, not wanting him considering her to be as crazy as she did.

LeeAnn prepared for the weekend as competently as she had had equipped the playroom. Bringing plenty of her sisters clothes, a list of their food allergies, telephone numbers of their pediatrician and the nearest emergency room, and their health insurance cards. Also six, one hundred dollar bills from their father: for casual expenses. Valerie didn't tell David this either. Being worn out from his part-time job, he insist on the children being invited every weekend.

The ride against traffic into New York City was peaceful and The Monsters napped in the back seat. Maybe they were tired from watching an early morning rerun of *Sex and the City*, Valerie thought. Fearing their reaction, LeeAnn hadn't told them that David's apartment lacked cable TV.

"You're telling Ralph *this* weekend?" Valerie demanded/asked.

LeeAnn took her right hand off the steering wheel and pointed with her thumb to the back seat. Since her left hand trailed out the window this made the car momentarily rudderless and Valerie wondered which of her parents had taught her to drive before concluding that it probably didn't matter.

"They're sleeping," Valerie said, trying to keep LeeAnn calm so they would reach the City alive.

"Sometimes they pretend."

Of course, Valerie thought, how could I not suspect this from members of her family. Then she changed the subject.

"Do you go to church?"

"We will after we're married," LeeAnn responded, turning her head. "Don't be so nervous. I only had one accident and it wasn't my fault. The driver should have gone into the mall like everyone does so when I turned left and he kept going straight he hit me."

"Did he signal that he was turning?"

"No one signals in Scarsdale."

Valerie felt thrown by LeeAnn's warped logic.

"What church do your parents go to?"

"None now. Originally the Anglican one till Mom turned onto its great looking minister."

"Do you miss it?"

"What's this religion kick?"

Valerie thought fast, knowing that she would get nowhere if LeeAnn felt that she was being pressured.

"David's half Jewish and I'm looking for somewhere we'd both feel comfortable."

"What are you?"

"Mom's Catholic, my father was a Methodist way back. Since we're passing it, I thought that we could stop on Twenty- ninth Street. The late minister there wrote a best seller on positive thinking." Then she added in feigned despair, "maybe David won't like it."

"OK, but just for a minute. I have to buy food."

"Where have you and Ralph been eating?"

"At home. Too many people would recognize him." Then she added in a low tone, "Besides, I like cooking for him."

Valerie strained against the shoulder harness as the car skidded onto the exit ramp off the Henry Hudson Parkway.

"You should slow down when leaving a highway," she said.

"I did." The speedometer read sixty two.

"Now!"

The tires screeched as LeeAnn abruptly slowed to thirty five.

"Car has anti-lock brakes and traction control," she said.

The Monsters continued sleeping or pretending to sleep, they apparently being used to her driving.

LeeAnn found a parking spot a block from the church. The four approached it silently. Valerie didn't know what else to say having used up her daily capacity for fantasy. While David *was* half-Jewish they'd probably elope. And forget about a honeymoon—the loft needed furniture. Valerie felt that things were moving too quickly for her. Maybe her interest in religion reflected *her* need to slow down. Deep in concentration, Valerie was saved from walking into a mailbox by a jerk on her hand.

"Watch it!" one of The Monsters warned. Valerie would pray to.

She did. The church was like any other, cool and nearly empty on an early Friday evening. Her charges quickly made annoyed comments, LeeAnn agreed to come another day and, with this faint promise, they returned to the car. LeeAnn bought the children ice cream at a tiny store they passed as reward for their religious exertion, emphasizing that it had to be finished before reentering the car. Obviously that was her spiritual home, Valerie thought.

David's condo was four blocks north of City Hall and could legally be owned only by artists. The owner, a friend of his father, was temporarily living in France while establishing a Paris gallery and had rented the apartment cheaply to David in exchange for care taking services.

Its initial renovations were informal and included a cement shower in an equally creative bathroom lacking doors, which David built. The cat in residence sometimes nursed at the bathtub fixture. No one had yet analyzed her behavior but Valerie was sure that The Monsters would.

They lived up to their nickname after learning that there wasn't cable TV. Taking turns bawling and screeching, they insisted on going home. Their behavior quickly exhausted Valerie's patience although LeeAnn remained calm.

"You don't *need* it. You have puzzles and crayons and games. David and Valerie *love* to play. They even have *a cat* and you know how much you always wanted one."

This information grabbed them and they scampered after the cat as it hid beneath the bed until they coaxed it out. Within moments the children were stroking her and the room became quiet. LeeAnn waited ten minutes, then left after embracing Valerie. For luck, she said.

Driving uptown, braless in the gray wool blend T-shirt, neck warmer, and beaded denim skirt from Madison Avenue's Max Mara, LeeAnn peeked into the mirror. She was pleased with what she saw but also felt scared to death. This was why she was driving so fast.

Fear made her impulsive and she vowed to control her feelings when speaking with Ralph who, she believed, loved her. Then what she recognized as her low self-esteem reasserted itself in a thought: what forty nine year old wouldn't love a teenager?

Her anxiety remained as she walked through the corner supermarket. Grabbing a grocery cart, she ignored the smile of a man older than Ralph who peeled off her sweater with his eyes. Though Ralph smoked and drank heavily, he insisted on healthy food so she chose salmon, spinach, fat-free cheese, and whole wheat bread. She bought virgin olive oil salad dressing from a gourmet shop across the street. Which wasn't as good as that from the Village's Balducci store, Ralph insisted, but it would do until they opened a branch store nearby.

Once in the apartment she put away the food and waited. The strain made her tired as she lay on the sofa. Though not intending to, she fell asleep. In her dream she was in labor, the baby lay sideways, and she felt enormous pain which the doctor couldn't relieve saying that he feared a drug would harm her child. She screamed and jerked awake during the first caesarean cut, only to find herself being held by Ralph.

"Did you fail an exam?" he asked.

"Sort of," she replied evasively. Her intention to tell him of her pregnancy as soon as they met evaporated and she wondered if she would ever have the courage. They ate, and he complimented her cooking. Then they had sex after showering together, this now being their ritual. She was relieved that her pregnancy still didn't show and wondered at his response when it did.

While watching the news from bed, like any couple, Ralph asked how teenagers thought. You'll be eighteen and voting soon."

"In twenty three months."

"What do you think about politicians?"

"Just a few are sexy," she replied, caressing his balls

under the blanket. Instead of being pleased, Ralph became annoyed. He liked women but was committed to politics. Sensing his seriousness, LeeAnn still held him but asked, "How do you mean?"

"Why would you vote for one politician rather than another?"

Remembering her vow against speaking impulsively, LeeAnn clenched her teeth and inadvertently squeezed. He jerked and she apologized, stating that she had been thinking hard. Then she lay primly in bed and pulled the blanket up to her neck.

Ralph rephrased his question. "Do your friends think about politics?"

"A few. About as many as dress grungy."

"What would make them enthusiastic about a politician?" Ralph knew how intensively corporations who sought the loyalty of adult customers marketed to youth.

Now LeeAnn did think.

"My friends regard politics as strategy. First fighting then compromise. Bargaining for small things is contemptible. Petty people seeking trivial things won't get our votes."

Ralph thought for several moments, then told LeeAnn one of Tower's stories, being interested in her reaction.

"A hundred years ago a famous congressman, Joe Cannon, was running for re-election. He asked a campaign worker whether he had been making mistakes and was told that people objected to his cursing. They wondered whether it was right to have a man with such a foul mouth representing their district. Cannon smiled and said that when he grew up everyone swore. Now it was a habit and didn't mean anything. Like the behavior of Brother Jones, a local preacher short on godliness who prayed continuously. Both don't mean a damned thing by it.'"

"But what we want is someone with vision who *does* believe," LeeAnn asserted, her eyes shining.

Ralph felt his penis harden as he experienced the most surprising desire of his life: that LeeAnn were older so they could marry.

BOOK TWO

DECEPTION TIMES THREE

Pride's Consequence

CHAPTER FOURTEEN

THEY MET IN a large brownstone on East Thirty-second Street, ten blocks from Grand Central Station. Early last century the building was the private residence of Emil Berlinger, a wealthy German-Jewish financier whose conversion to Christianity didn't enable him to buy property in the more exclusive area two miles north. After he and his wife died their only child, Erich, a psychiatrist and one of New York's first psychoanalysts, lived and conducted his practice in this building. After being rejected for a teaching post because of anti-Semitism, he re-embraced his Jewish faith and fled to Texas, there quickly gaining state licensing and a medical school appointment. Soon he married the daughter of a Presbyterian minister who, wanting family unity, converted to Judaism, a faith considered exotic and not reprehensible by their neighbors.

Upon moving, Dr. Berlinger took only his clothes and books, selling the mansion and its contents to a major American University for its alumni headquarters. Seeking a homelike atmosphere, the architect used these furnishings wherever possible, they thereafter becoming cherished by generations of alumni and remaining through renovations. Thus it was that early one morning in late May a tall blond man stood before the wall of one of the club's smaller meeting rooms, being amazed by Emil Berlinger's baptism certificate and motive for it which were described in paragraphs beneath its frame.

The man had joined the club six years earlier after learning of its lax membership requirements. Faced with mounting financial difficulty many alumni organizations had merged and this building was now the New York City headquarters for twenty three American and fourteen foreign schools. Although membership information was never checked, the man had studied a course catalog from his alleged year of graduation and visited the school to learn landmarks.   He was very cautious. He also felt disturbed that so intelligent a man as Berlinger should have considered the parochialism of others.

He himself held no prejudice. Concerned only with competence, he was uninterested in his colleagues' demographics although he did object to some personalities. He disliked sadistic and violent people but needed both in his work. Also, unclean clothes and bodies and poor table manners but he tolerated these. He disliked obesity too though he had once loved a woman who was seventy pounds overweight. He tried to be open-minded.

While waiting, the man considered his life, though he was convinced that emotions inhibited logical thinking and always feared the errors which they might foster. And, although raised Christian, he considered altruism to be the least worthy virtue.

His most unselfish deed was to protect his alcoholic stepmother from the wrath of his father after she left unattended his ill half-sister. This caused the accidental death of his father. Her lies in court sealed his fate: removed him as heir of the family business; ended contact with his sister; and sent him to Devonmere Adolescent Correctional Center whose rigors, though termed "treatment," were more greatly feared than those of neighboring Dartmoor Prison.

He was terrified when he entered the Correctional Center at fifteen. Upon leaving it at twenty-one, he feared nothing. No more could be done to him, no more taken away. Only his intelligence and rage, first exhibited and then deeply hidden, enabled his survival.

In his first month he lived in a room which differed from those of inexpensive motels largely by its peephole, locked door, and light which remained on, for the staff feared that he would attempt suicide. Then his roommate did. Trying to conceal their incompetence, the guards accused him of a second killing and fabricated arguments between cell mates. No indictment resulted but thereafter he was treated as if he were incorrigible, his knowledge of the guards' corruption fueling their behavior. Beatings, solitary confinement, and forced association with sadistic inmates filled many of his days until his release.

But he learned much. The last of his cell mates, having set fire to a schoolroom in which his hated teacher was locked, sensed an affinity between them and instructed him as they exercised. The man learned how to harm others; why ingenious crimes failed. And, although female prisoners were isolated separately, the need to be wary of women, a lesson which he already learned. Shortly before his release this friend was murdered and the man learned his most important lesson: to trust only in himself.

The man left Devonmere with two conclusions: that well-planned crimes promised great reward with little risk; and that the criminal world was changing into a knowledge based economy with intermediaries being essential for success.

` To gain initial working capital, the man took the most promising job which the Labour Exchange offered: as trucker's helper for a computer chip manufacturer in Manchester. After five months of diligent work, and following heavy drinking during a Liverpool football match between the Reds and Sky Blues (Liverpool vs. Coventry City), the driver accepted his helper's offer to complete delivery while he slept. He was later to be picked up by the helper on his return from Plymouth.

Both helper and cargo vanished. Selling the goods presented no problem since only much later were these parts stamped with serial numbers. Through brokers they were eventually purchased by Taiwan manufacturers for products sold in the United States.

This, the first major such theft, resulted in computer shipping security being improved and he acquiring one million four hundred thousand pounds.

The man moved to Dundalk, a small city in the Irish Republic forty miles from the border with Northern Ireland. Here he gained another conclusion which further molded his career: that political ideology motivated people to spend enormous sums.

Buying a small house on the outskirts of town, he described himself as the wealthy university dropout he might once have become and settled into the community.

The man spent evenings in a pub but spoke frequently with only one man: a semi-retired seventy four year old priest who truly loved people and had great tolerance for human frailty, attitudes which the man found unfathomable.

As he grew older the man adopted the title of Major, causing others to assume his military experience though, because of his background, no country's armed forces would accept him. A guerrilla leader once offered him this honorary rank. The man readily accepted this compliment for he considered discourtesy to be reprehensible.

This man, The Major, ended his self-reflection as his three hired consultants began arriving, in staggered ten minute intervals. Food and drink awaited them. These were tests for the man regarded lateness, gluttony, and drunkenness as unacceptable for his employees as would a corporate manager. But their behavior, considering their professions, would likely be conservative.

All these experts were unknown to each other. Their contract was with a business incorporated in

Liechtenstein, Advanced Knowledge and Technology Limited. This was his current designation, which changed frequently. It always consisted of him, the usual puppet attorney/shareholder, mail/fax/e-mail addresses, and a telephone number answered by a highly paid multi-lingual grandmother with an amazingly seductive voice who serviced hundreds of similar companies.

His business was always profitable and his savings had achieved such a level (twenty nine million dollars) that money no longer influenced his activity. He worked because he enjoyed it more than anything else he might do, possibly even sex. A conclusion which he regarded with concern for he knew that this wasn't healthy. Despite the danger of his work the man pursued a cautious lifestyle.

The door opened and The Major greeted his first arrival. That Gerald was six minutes early possibly reflected his minimal unconscious resistance to externally imposed structure. A tolerable characteristic considering his great competence.

After his termination, because of university politics, from a post in biochemistry at Bristol University, Gerald turned his intelligence to the options market, quickly losing three million pounds and gaining an indictment for fraud. Seeking a psychiatric defense, he consulted a doctor who informed The Major of Gerald's predicament. A skillful lawyer was recommended, favors were employed, and all charges were dropped. Following his mandated treatment,

Gerald entered a more rewarding profession: advising The Major, indirectly, on the latest developments in chemical and biological warfare.

Heinz and Calvin arrived exactly at their designated times. Heinz had the broadest education, holding doctorates in law and physics from Ludwig-Maximilians University in Munich. The repentant son of an unapologetic Gestapo official who received a state funeral in Syria, Heinz, after studying his father's deeds, converted to Judaism and married an Israeli.

Though long divorced, he being too used to the submissive nature of German women for this marriage to be successful, they still maintained contact and he visited Israel yearly. He even occasionally wore a skullcap, which The Major regretted though not on religious grounds: a six foot five inch blond man capped by black wool was too unusual a sight for Frankfurt.

Calvin's background was the most traditional. The son of an American army general, he held a doctorate in political science and taught international affairs at Yale University. His most recent book, on the diversification and globalization of the defense industry, was little appreciated by his department's promotion committee which refused his appointment to full professor. Many related this to their hostility to *anything* military. The extraordinary cost of his autistic son's treatment motivated Calvin for this well paid assignment.

The meeting began. To avoid interruption, The Major had arranged for food in warming trays to be ready at their arrival. He ordered what *he* liked (after reminding himself that they were *his* employees): shrimp cocktail, mozzarella and tomato salad with basil and cracked peppercorns, roasted fillet of salmon, breast of chicken, pasta with spinach and ricotta, a carafe of Valpolicella Valpantena, Secco Bertani 1992, coffee and (a *must* in New York City) cheesecake. As he expected, and to his satisfaction, the wine remained untouched.

After introducing the men by aliases, he briefly described their fields and asked that they remain anonymous. They readily agreed. College professors enjoy considering themselves romantic and mysterious, disciples of Dr. Kissinger. After food was selected and all were again seated, he began his well practiced speech.

"We've hired you because this project demands the best. It will take no more than five days of your time for which you're being well paid. I've arranged rooms for you here and in each of your packets is an envelope containing five thousand dollars for incidental expenses, I think you'll agree that the amount is generous but we find that creative people are capable of their greatest productivity when they are unburdened by minor frustrations."

He knew that his words were a bit much but also that one could never flatter academicians too greatly nor overestimate their gullibility.

"How vulnerable are nations to terrorism? *Now!* Still greatly, we believe, even after the World Trade Centers destruction—yet we don't know for sure. The anonymity of terror groups and their orientation towards pockets of opportunity make this difficult to assess. If there is a 'fog of war' there is also a 'smog of terrorism.' When assessing a conventional army we analyze communication intercepts and make predictions based on their known doctrine and strategy. Something which is not possible with isolated groups whose motives may be vague, criminal, or intended to effect a punitive action and publicize a cause. Their fluid or unknown ideology hinders our recognition of potential dangers.

"Even now we must think the unthinkable: new weapons and scenarios for destruction are being developed. These create difficulty in protecting civilized nations from rogues. How many of you still long for the good old days when we could blame Moscow for bombings and assorted mayhem?"

The Major didn't expect a show of hands from these sophisticates but he did get the relaxed smiles he had anticipated.

"I began with the general question of how vulnerable nations are to terrorism. Our task is to determine how vulnerable America is *today*, by considering the international environment, technological changes, and terrorist motivation. Then to create so viable and diabolical a plan that Americans will *demand* that their representatives activate *permanent* protective structures. Unlike those which were so unwisely relaxed last year. I can state this. The Pentagon cannot. But this outcome will earn your exorbitant fees many times over."

He added a wry smile to his last sentence in which, as he expected, they joined. The one hundred sixty five thousand dollars which each was being paid was but two percent of the amount which had been wired into his account forty days earlier. The Major's enthusiasm was contagious and none raised embarrassing questions.

Setting a huge fee and technical challenge had the effect of placing fragrant ham before a starving dog: focusing attention and ignoring other considerations. He knew that congressional action was certain—but only after the horrific plan which they devised was successful.

CHAPTER FIFTEEN

THE MAJOR PERMITTED the experts to bond while they shared stories of subtle academic politics. He then turned the discussion to their task by relating amusing anecdotes of terrorism from a more structured age.

The Baader-Meinhof gang leaders who sought money from well-heeled sympathizers to lead a comfortable consumer life; and Juliane Plambeck's claim to notoriety before becoming a murderer, she being described by comrades as "the trophy for the erotic challenge cup."

Then, lest they lose focus, he detailed the tragic killing of the influential German banker, Juergen Ponto, by the goddaughter he loved like his own child. Half of the German terrorists in the nineteen eighties were young, well educated women.

He adjourned the meeting at ten-thirty after stating that deliberations would begin promptly at eight on the following morning and were governed by the American secrecy laws which would be rigorously enforced by all NATO nations; that meals would be communal and held in the meeting room; and that dates with local women should be scheduled *after* eleven at night. As he expected, they smiled at his allusion to their desired romantic natures, and quietly left the room.

Before going to sleep The Major set his alarm for five to give himself time to walk, this being when his most creative ideas often occurred. Then, checking his laptop, he found two messages.

The first, unsigned, read: "It's better in the Bahamas." Well-intentioned advice from a past collaborator, using words plagiarized from Meyer Lansky who had used that country as a transshipment center for organized crime's vast fortunes.

The second message was from Father Brian, his elderly but technologically adept Irish neighbor. It described a current scandal: school funds being used to finance a Paris conference for the staff. Then his ambivalence over the proposed change in the Abortion Law, ending with lines which lingered in The Major's mind as he fell asleep:

"We are born helpless then, becoming conscious, discover loneliness. We need others if we are to know anything, even ourselves. Sleep well my son."

CHAPTER SIXTEEN

Video recorders were activated before the group entered the room. The explanation which The Major gave, that it was to justify their fees, was readily accepted. In reality the tapes were to insure their silence after the catastrophe which they were about to devise occurred.

Deliberation began. Despite his frequent expressions of agitated enthusiasm The Major found their early hours together tedious. He had no interest in hearing a rambling history of terrorism, needing only a detailed plan and quick education to address his employer's concerns.

These men were knowledgeable; so were others he might have chosen. But each organized well and was a superb teacher. Several had given *simplified* technical workshops. A year before, one corporate president raved that after a seven hour session he really understood Cost-effective Telecommunications Management, including the distinction between extended Erlang B and C, and time division multiplexing. And both he and The Major were only high school graduates!

So The Major listened and kept disagreements from escalating into walkout—which could occur when academicians became overheated. Though this was unlikely here since it would mean forfeiting their huge fees.

Heinz, exhibiting the German love for English authors, quoted Conrad's novel, *The Secret Agent*. All recognized the validity of this writer's words even a hundred years later, when terrorists mouthed the same philosophy.

"It is this country which is dangerous with her idealistic conceptions of legality...to break up the superstition and worship of legality should be our aim. Nothing would please me more than to see Inspector Heat and his likes take to shooting us down in broad daylight with the approval of the public. Half our battle would be won...the disintegration of the old morality would have set in its very temple."

Heinz, with a gesture of good feeling, then yielded the floor to Calvin. Who made the obvious statement that the introduction of more effective weapons than the revolver and bomb of the nineteenth century made terrorism more deadly. The tiny Czech machine pistol, Skorpion VZ61, whose silencer spreads the shots making hits more probable. The M-26 grenade, a large number of which were stolen in nineteen seventy one from a US Army base in Miesau, Germany, particularly deadly in crowds. The RPG-7 portable rocket launcher which, though of poor accuracy, is easy to fire and does extraordinary damage.

Gerald looked as bored as The Major felt. The most technically minded of the three (though Heinz was trained in physics), Gerald appeared to be following the discussion despite spending most of his time looking at his coffee, to which he periodically added more Splenda non-caloric sweetener.

By noon of their first day the deeds and philosophies of major terrorists had been dissected. Fanon's belief that violence was beneficial for it freed the masses of their sense of impotence and enabled them to understand social truths. Marighella's widely read *Handbook Of Urban Guerrilla Warfare* which was closely studied by the Baader-Meinhof gang. The propaganda coup of the Symbionese Liberation Army in its kidnapping of nineteen year old Patricia Hearst, daughter of newspaper magnate William Randolph Hearst. The failure of the Guevara cult in South America which, aided by the nihilistic philosophies of Debray and Marcuse, led to irregular forces being transformed into the urban terrorists of today. An odd development since Guevara had long warned of the folly of terrorism in contrast to guerrilla warfare.

Thirty minutes were spent analyzing the deeds of "Carlos" (Ilich Ramirez Sanchez) whose great intelligence and ability to combine enemies with differing motives were described as his major strengths by Sheik Yamani, a rare captive who lived to share their conversation. Calvin considered Carlos to be the first postmodern terrorist, one without philosophy and willing to sell his expertise for the right price.

The Major, though believing that Carlos' present residence in a French prison benefited the world community, recognized their similarity. And he feared, despite his precautions, of becoming as publicly known.

Though he had scheduled the day's session through eight, The Major felt that all needed a break and dismissed his charges after lunch. They responded like school children being surprised with a holiday.

The Major hadn't visited New York City in twenty years and wondered if he would remember any sights as he walked to evaluate suitable targets.

Would destruction of another building or the loss of life serve best? While inflicting mass casualties usually harms a terrorist's cause it does exemplify power. But the political need to retaliate would be enormous and the United States, having finally shaken off the effects of its impotence in Vietnam, would adopt a war mentality and destroy all who were even remotely involved. He was alone and could disappear but what of his unknown employer who might have loved ones. He didn't know their identity but there were many possibilities.

The two hundred year domination of the state system was under siege from many quarters. Countries using terrorism as a form of diplomacy. Groups governed by religious and tribal loyalties promising security in this rapidly changing, threatening world. Drug cartels and other criminal enterprises seeking to increase and secure their profits through political power. The lines between state, rogue state, and crime were becoming blurred. So The Major was convinced that he would continue to prosper.

What would have the greatest impact? Destruction once again of part, or all of this city? And could the death of ten thousand create the same effect as that of a hundred thousand in this land whose citizenry convulsed when a single (*white*) child's life was threatened. Perhaps destroying the Black ghetto of Harlem would gain the same result yet not risk the massive retaliation if the affluent East Side were laid waste. *Unless* politicians, after acquiescing to terrorist demands, could blame some native fringe movement. Anti-abortion Right-To-Lifers? Environmentalists? He smiled as he thought this, believing that his employer would find the suggestion amusing, and possibly useful.

CHAPTER SEVENTEEN

THE THIRD DAY'S meeting began. All except The Major were relaxed. Heinz' dress (cowboy shirt, jeans, carved Western boots, embroidered black and gold skullcap), which had been purchased on Ludlow Street the previous evening, produced smiles which he ignored.

"We don't need an elaborate plan. Just any, and the motivation to carry it out," Heinz said.

"How so?" Calvin asked.

"The security of most cities and industrial plants is inept and far from casino standards: police without machine pistols; overweight guards who can barely walk and without shoot-to-kill orders even in nuclear bomb assembly facilities."

All who were present identified with his sarcastic tone, knowing of the study in which coed nuclear plant guards were described as being "great for a department store"—when they weren't practicing quick draw with loaded guns or exchanging sexual favors.

"The emotional factor is more important," Gerald interjected. "The greatest effect of terrorism is appearance not reality. More people are killed by auto crashes than bombs in Northern Ireland but which frightens people more? Terrorism *can* be defended against but people become angry when their ordered lives are interrupted. The *will* to defend is lacking."

"Which is our task," The Major said. "To produce a plan so terrifying that it will *inject* backbone into America's elected representatives."

The Major repeatedly emphasized their working goal for he feared that the group would sense its basic illogic. That *their* lack of security more characterized a market research investigation than a secret government study. Another of his concerns (the boss should worry the most, his father had always advised) was that they were *too* relaxed, too greatly enjoying their interlude from academic and family responsibilities. Anxious that the conference would end without result, this reducing his reputation and likely longevity, he thought of how he might goad them. Then, while viewing Gerald refuse the tray of Danish pastry and add another Splenda to his coffee, an idea popped into his mind: motivate them with fear. But how?

He remembered his notes about them. All led sedentary lives. Heinz' adventurousness was reflected in his provocative (still, to some Germans) wearing of yarmulke. Calvin and his family lived in faculty housing near the university. Gerald loved roses. He doubted the threat to destroy a satellite TV link-up or garden would motivate their creativity yet, what if...

The Major's serious tone aroused them. "I received word this morning of an event which may affect our deliberation but is being kept quiet to avoid panic. Seventy four Jewish children and teachers, waiting outside a Hebrew School in Bremen, were sprayed with a gun similar to an Israeli Model 5 tear gas dispenser. Thirty one are dead. The rest have neurological and respiratory symptoms and remain in guarded condition. A letter taking responsibility by the Wehrsportgruppe Hoffman* was received. CSIS** is aiding the investigation."

All knew of this group whose past actions included a bombing which killed twelve and wounded hundreds in Munich. Hoffman was arrested following the murder of a Jewish publisher.

Gerald continued sipping his coffee. The others shook their heads.

"I thought they were gone," Heinz said. "Down to under a hundred since the eighties. Madness."

"They've never known war and view it as entertainment," Calvin added.

The next scheduled topic, the motivation and training of terrorists, was shelved to concentrate on *the plan*, a change which The Major viewed with quiet satisfaction.

Such widely feared events as atomic detonation or poisoning the water supply were quickly dismissed. "Going nuclear" was technically too difficult, while to effectively poison a major city's water supply would require hundreds of tons of agent.

*A banned German neo-Nazi, anti-Semitic terrorist group
**Georgetown Center for Strategic and International Studies

Discussion raged until dinner without result and The Major feared that none would appear. Despite the deadline he suggested that they adjourn early and sleep on the problem. All were upset by news of the Bremen attack and they somberly agreed.

Hoping for a breakthrough, The Major walked south along Lexington Avenue. Despite his role in its next catastrophe he loved New York City for its varied nationalities and frantic pace reminded him of his youthful travels through London where he lived in an adult world.

After his mother's accidental death when he was three, from the almost incomprehensible conjunction of shock from a toaster's electrical defect and her undiagnosed heart problem, his father feared losing him too. So, thereafter, he was tutored at home when not accompanying his father on business trips.

Most children play with toy guns. His were the real weapons which his father sold: tanks, machine guns, rifles. All for a good price, cash or barter.

The business, Jasper Daye & Son, was begun by his grandfather who, having little expectation of permanent peace following World War Two, bought surplus military supplies from both Eastern and Western bloc nations. Then he sold these to revolutionary movements using phony end-user certificates and bills of lading, and to legal but threatened governments.

His ideology consisted of three beliefs. Work should be fun. Be frugal with business expenses but generous with wages. Agreements must be honored. His father had lived these convictions and so did he.

The Major walked aimlessly, awaiting an idea. For whatever reason he turned east at Twenty-ninth Street and found himself before a window filled with toy soldiers. Expensive ones for adults who play war games, costing at least ninety dollars each. His father purchased these by mail and the address must have lingered in his memory.

He stared intently into the window display, remembering. A concerned store clerk watched but then turned back to his work: the stranger was too well dressed to cause problems.

Minutes passed. Then, while viewing the figures of a nineteenth century nurse and wounded drummer boy, the idea of a plan came to him. An event so diabolical as to bring America to its knees and well earn his fee. One to brighten the face of his employer, whoever they might be. He didn't know if the scheme was possible. But his three professors would.

CHAPTER EIGHTEEN

THE MAJOR RETURNED, feeling convinced that the group would accept his horror only if it came from them. Luckily, Gerald was lingering in the Library. A misnomer since it held only the *New York Times*, *Wall Street Journal*, alumni newspapers, and cheaply discarded early twentieth century novels.

The Major sat in an adjoining chair and waited. Gerald's eyes were glassy and The Major wondered how much he had drunk. This was significant in view of his usual healthy habits. Finally Gerald spoke, with good self-control.

"Depressing."

The Major remained silent, awaiting more.

"What do you think?"

The Major adopted a naive tone. "The study was a good idea. Though if it doesn't cause outcry..."

"Now only the unusual would, something based on a primary fear," instructed Gerald.

The Major's tone became encouraging as their ideas merged.

"I think you're onto something. Not another plane crash into a building or even a bombing. But something to arouse horror from deep in the unconscious. A fire? Burn police stations to arouse social chaos?"

This inadequate suggestion achieved its expected response.

Gerald shifted in his seat with eyes no longer dull. The scientist pondering a problem with an unsophisticated student.

"What alarmed you most in childhood?"

The Major saw no reason not to be honest.

"Losing my father. My mother was already dead."

"The remaining person to whom you were symbiotically tied. When did your fear leave?"

Never, The Major thought. But he didn't want to be transparent: sometimes he still feared being alone. "When I saw him again."

"And if he never returned?"

It hadn't taken long and The Major wondered if there were similar elements in their personalities.

"Terror."

"So great as would permanently wound a nation. How?"

Tired of playing his role, The Major spoke directly. "By killing mother *and* infant. From breaking her symbiotic tie to the child when she dies, and effecting her husband more profoundly after the death of both." They knew that Americans exalted mothers and children.

"Correct." Gerald looked pleased: the riddle was solved. The Major, also satisfied, was disappointed in how willingly a scientist would pervert his knowledge. But he knew that many academicians were contemptuous of those with lesser intelligence.

The Major came late to the next meeting, wanting to give Gerald time to share his (induced) brainstorm. After jibes about his "romantic evening," The Major said, "Before we begin, two more children have died." Then, "Any ideas for our plan?"

Gerald idea was quickly described and accepted. They spent the rest of the hour discussing its investigation.

"I'll research this on the Internet," Gerald volunteered, "but the plan seems workable. The physiology of pregnant and nursing mothers is unique. There should be a biological agent to effect it."

"Within what geographical area are we thinking? How will it be introduced?" asked Calvin, reflecting his expertise.

The work was divided. Gerald would identify the germ and devise its manufacture. Calvin, collaborating with him, would determine its method of dissemination. Heinz and The Major would find suitable targets within the City. The meeting then adjourned to permit independent research, with preliminary conclusions to be shared on the following day.

CHAPTER NINETEEN

THE MAJOR WALKED while his professors studied. He knew that his role, now peripheral, was still critical: to keep them working cooperatively, and prevent analysis of the project itself. His father once said, during one risky, simultaneous sale of arms to a country's legal *and* rebel forces, that busy hands didn't have time to think, this being was why soldiers were kept continuously occupied before a dangerous mission. So he would keep his professors absorbed, motivated by news of more Bremen casualties or another of his fantasies.

His employer had demanded that the plan be paralyzing in horror, untraceable, and all knowing of it be eliminated. The Major objected. Multiple deaths would arouse attention and be riskier than depending on their natural instinct for survival. Would any prosecutor, under enormous pressure to succeed, believe that such intelligent people would accept huge sums without knowing the real intent of their work? They would be lucky to get consecutive life sentences.

Silence would be their best defense. Particularly after they received an edited videotape of one of their meetings. Thereafter, their families would be grateful for the fortunate timing of their New York City visit, *well before* the catastrophe occurred. They would convince themselves that the terror was only *similar* to their plan, which certainly could not have worked. It was even possible that one of them would even be invited to join the commission investigating it. Deep in thought, The Major almost collided with a mother. He apologized, praised her child, and then wondered if they would be within the target area he hoped to define that day.

Again trusting his instincts, he walked towards the Empire State building. But he quickly dismissed this as a target, knowing that his employer wanted something different. He wondered if their motivation was money or hatred, the visceral quality of his instructions suggesting the latter.

He had initially considered their unsigned letter to be a prank. Until he claimed the five thousand, one hundred dollar bills, packed in two suitcases, which were left for him in the Dublin train station checkroom. He took their next letter seriously and complete payment was prompt. Like with his father, who was always paid in advance by men who wouldn't tolerate failure. Nor, likely, would his employer.

Reaching Fourteenth Street, he dismissed the huge apartment complex of Stuyvesant Town as being too narrow a target and continued walking. The area changed as he entered the impoverished East Village: a place of motorcycle gangs and drug dealers.

Driven by New York City's continuing crush for housing, he wondered how long it would be before the local Hells Angels' chapter opened a boutique selling wooden models of motorcycles to ecologically correct parents. This area *was* a possibility. But would people care deeply enough? They might blame addicts for the devastation and welcome its certain result: renovation followed by the construction of luxury apartments, not fear.

At Ninth Street he turned west, then south along Broadway, again following his instinct or something which he had been told. Here the buildings, though higher, had the ornate facades typical of nineteenth and early twentieth century structures. Once stores and factories, they now held publishing companies, government offices and court houses. Even, surprisingly, *families*.

During the recent glut of office space many buildings had been renovated into apartments close by powerful American institutions: the Stock Exchanges and Federal Reserve Bank.

His employers wanted an example not a war. If a serious biological attack killed millions he assumed that his goal was in the thousands. The downtown Broadway/Wall Street area was deserted at night except for its few residents and workers rebuilding the World Trade Centers.

The trick would be to contain the microbe—if something highly contagious could be. And it *must* be infectious for how otherwise could it spread. A contained contagious disease lethal only to women and children? Like the little bit pregnant conundrum, it seemed impossible even as a solution slipped through his mind. But he knew it would return when it was ripe. Hopefully while he still had consultants to validate it.

Though not hungry, The Major reminded himself it was lunch time and sought a restaurant with the low-fat meals he preferred, wondering why he had begun following this craze long before it became popular even in America. A corner fish restaurant from which he could watch passersby seemed ideal and he was soon enjoying the grilled tuna which he ordered whenever it was available.

Remembering his father's warning, to never confuse activity with progress, he wrote words on a pad: *mothers, infants, lethal, contained.* Then he circled each.

How to contain it? To genetically engineer a new agent was too time-consuming and required great facilities. Moreover, could one be made? Must the germ be contagious or just well spread? The problem was extraordinary. And probably, he reflected, why he was being so well paid.

Deep in thought, he spilled the once daily glass of wine which he permitted himself. While keeping the stain from spreading, the solution again popped into his mind. So natural that it was maybe the only one. He remembered reading that Einstein had once described Piaget's revolutionary explanation of children's thinking as being so simple that only a genius could have thought of it. Though not considering himself more than clever, The Major would have enjoyed trying to hire Einstein or Piaget.

CHAPTER TWENTY

THEY WERE BEING difficult: obsessing about unimportant elements of the plan. Which wasn't what The Major wanted. Maybe eliminating them *was* a good idea, he thought. Until he remembered another of his father's morals, told after he knocked an erring employee into a wall.

"Behaving impulsively isn't smart. Now he's my enemy. I should have explained softly."

He apologized to the worker, paid for his wife's pregnancy, and gave him a raise. Then he took him to lunch where both laughed about the incident. But he never trusted him again and arranged for his hire at a better paying job with a nearby business he secretly owned. Twenty years later The Major recalled what his father meant: losing your temper could be expensive.

Modifying smallpox's DNA was on Gerald's mind during another of his rambling stories. Any other time The Major, who loved learning for its own sake, would have listened with interest. Now, as each minute led towards the conference's conclusion without a viable plan, he wanted to rip out Gerald's tongue. Or, preferably, to break his leg, to motivate his more productive speech.

"You know of Watson and Crick?" Gerald asked, in the relaxed manner of underworked tenured professors. Unfortunately, Calvin didn't. The Major looked raptly and thought of squeezing Gerald's balls.

"Why do blue-eyed parents have a blue-eyed child?" he began. "How can a bacterium suddenly develop the capacity to survive at a higher temperature than normal for its species? *Mendel* you would say with your limited, high school knowledge: some genes are dominant, others recessive. Yes. But how is the genetic information passed along by the cells?

"We didn't know until fifty years ago when Oswald Avery at the Rockefeller Institute demonstrated that if a *specific* molecule found in all living cells was destroyed the organism could no longer pass on its genes. This was DNA —I wont bore you with its long name."

One hard squeeze on his balls, The Major thought, though his expression remained engrossed.

"Ten years later Rosalind Franklin at Kings College, London, discovered that the molecule was made of five key chemicals. Cambridge's Watson and Crick figured it out. One of the chemicals formed a winding ladder with rungs made of the other four. When deciphered, they revealed the secrets of life!"

Despite his impatience The Major became fascinated, sensing a useful connection between Gerald's information and something he had read. The key to their problem: a factor toxic only to pregnant women and infants. He listened closely. Again his father was proven right and he mourned his loss.

"DNA and its sister compound RNA are the universal codes by which bacterium and viruses produce others. Genes create traits and these are sections of them.

"Viruses are marked by noting their differences through an electron microscope, or their response to the body's immune system. They have proteins to invade our cells and we have antibodies to destroy them. Salk used the antibody response against the outer proteins of the polio virus in his vaccine. Since penicillin was discovered we have had lethal cocktails for bacteria. But some have special characteristics in their DNA and can outwit antibiotics using their "R" or resistance factors, which makes smallpox such a valuable weapon.

"Consider its characteristics. Smallpox *loves* people. It killed more of them than any other virus. You inhale a particle and feel fine. But days later you get a backache and take aspirin. Then you have a little fever and, soon, terrible dreams. Nothing serious you tell yourself, but..."

Gerald paused dramatically. All stopped eating.

"Tiny red spots appear, like those older people get. They become blisters engorged with pus, and turn into hard sacs. The skin splits. You can't speak or open your eyes but you know everything until you die from a heart attack. Or you live with the characteristic pocks. Though there's a smallpox no one survives. The skin stays smooth but blackens and slips off the body in sheets, blood oozing from all openings. It's diagnosed by smell."

Claude's face became pasty as Gerald made his point.

"Why trouble to devise something special when the smallpox virus is unmatched? Three hundred million dead from it in this century alone. And it still exists in many labs despite lies that it was destroyed in all but two. A plan incorporating this would rouse people to fund *all* countermeasures."

This was something which The Major did consider but his instructions were specific. Smallpox was too contagious and inelegant. A warning was desired, not the overreaction to a catastrophe.

But how to explain this without elaborating.

Needing his own pause, The Major took a sip of wine. So did all except Gerald.

"Smallpox would be *too* terrifying," The Major said finally. "We want people to demand action, not become immobilized. Threaten too greatly and they'll push their heads deeper into the sand. Like those who ignore all warnings about food, believing that if so many aren't healthy then one may as well eat everything."

He hoped that they found this explanation satisfactory, being unable to think of another.

It worked because Gerald didn't really care about the issue, his brief technical lecture just being intended to put the non-academician employer in his place.

The Major still couldn't remember what he sensed would solve their problem. Then, hoping to rouse his staff from the depression induced by Gerald's graphic recitation, he wished them a romantically successful evening although believing that they would, as usual, be watching TV. As he spoke, two words jumped from his unconscious.

"What's the TSS hypothesis?"

Gerald preened like any expert being asked to provide an explanation. "Full or summary description?"

"As much as we have time for without imposing on your evening."

Gerald sprawled, loosened his tie and opened his collar (a first for him), then looked about the group.

"Men's discomfort with normal functions. That's what started it. How to keep women productive in the office and factory when, for days every month, they worry about the embarrassment of odor and blood stain. Ancient cultures kept menstruating women isolated but this is hardly a practical solution for an expanding economy. The Romans used wool inserts; the Japanese, rolled paper tubes; the Americans, rags. None were ideal.

"In the nineteen thirties a Colorado physician invented the familiar tube within a tube. Then he sold his patent to Tampax which cornered ninety percent of the tampon market. Sales were unregulated and they were never tested for safety.

"Intense competition drove manufacturers to a frenzy. To distinguish their product as superior they used advertising which preyed on women's fears about odor or leakage. Feminists insisted that women could function as well as men in all jobs: fire-fighter or news anchor. No one could afford embarrassment. Additions were made to the basic tampon. In the nineteen seventies synthetic fibers and plastics took the place of cotton and cardboard.

"A super absorbent tampon was made of highly compressed beads of polyester and cellulose. It was capable of absorbing twenty times its weight and marketed as the product which a woman could rely on. So it was named *Rely*. Many manufacturers made similar products.

"But problems developed. As the tampon swelled, dryness occurred. Also pain, when it adhered to and tore cells from the vaginal wall. Some tampons expanded so much that they couldn't be removed. Still, no one questioned their use despite there having been warning signs: lesions were being produced on tissue in rabbits, and the cellulose was proving ideal for bacterial toxins.

"Then doctors in a college town noticed something scary. A sudden increase in toxic shock syndrome cases, and not just in women. Men and children too, though most of the early cases were menstruating adolescents. The symptoms were high fever, vomiting, diarrhea, kidney dysfunction, liver failure, platelet formation, shedding of skin cells, confusion. Finally, death. All were infected with *Staphylococcus aureus,* which was resistant to penicillin antibiotics and secreted an unusual toxin.

"A Japanese pediatrician, Kawasaki, treated children having a staphylococcal infection causing skin shedding, heart infections, and the loss of toes and fingers. The illness wasn't new. Rare cases dated back fifty years. But these were increasing and ninety five percent of the patients were females who became ill several days into their periods. Most used the new super absorbent tampons. Everyone panicked and companies spent millions advertising *not* to use them."

Gerald paused dramatically. Then he gave his punch line.

"But all of the scientists were wrong and refused to believe the one immunologist, Schlievert, who was right. A doctor sent him blood for analysis from someone suffering from an odd case of Kawasaki syndrome. Schlievert found a new type of streptococcal poison in the patient's blood, a 'pyrogenic exotoxin' or fever producing poison.

"The first infection produced a mild reaction, the second or third during succeeding menstrual cycles, a massive one. The auto immune system self-destructs as this particular staph strain, toxic shock syndrome toxin-1 or TSST-1, generated two thousand times faster than normal.

"A single milligram could kill a two hundred pound man by producing chaos in his immune system, massively increasing the CD4 T-cell population. If this sounds familiar it is because they are destroyed by the

AIDS virus. Without doubt TSST-1 is the most potent immune system stimulator ever found. A super antigen.

"So the tampon wasn't the problem but a factor. Getting rid of them wouldn't eliminate the illness: the organism would adapt by finding another growth site. What caused its resistance to penicillin? It produces an enzyme, beta-lactamase, rendering the drug harmless.

Doctors did have alternative medicines. Methicillin. Naficillin. Cephalosporins. The surefire staph killer Vancomycin. All worked for awhile against this bug, which is everywhere but harmless. *Unless* it finds a cut, or immune stressed person: a pregnant woman, an infant, a hospitalized person; children with bruises and unwashed hands wiping their noses."

The Major perked up: his problem was solved. Now to get his professors on board.

CHAPTER TWENTY ONE

G<small>ERALD</small> <small>CONTINUED</small> <small>TELLING</small> stories the next day but The Major didn't intervene for he sensed that progress was being made.

"Some viruses duplicate slowly and repair their genetic material. Others resort chromosomes, shift their RNA almost randomly. Take the bluetongue virus..."

The non-technologist Calvin rolled his eyes, which the rest ignored.

"A single mosquito can be easily infected with *two* strains and inject into animals a combination of both. That's unimportant you say—not many cattle live in Manhattan." His attempt at humor still aroused courteous smiles.

"Then take Russia in 1992. An encephalitis epidemic infected a hundred thousand people. This was caused by a gene swap between the Inkoo and Tahyna viruses. Each is mild, producing little more than flu-like symptoms. But they become deadly after recombination. Microbes are outstanding genetic engineers. In one study, three percent of the time lab workers used a crippled virus to carry genes into other, hopefully improved plant cells, *new deadly species were produced.*

"That's deliberate you say. What about HIV/AIDS. Its RNA changes significantly one out of a thousand viral replications with millions occurring in each infected person every second. Maybe AIDS will develop the ability to infect lung cells and become a *respiratory* disease."

The resultant gasp produced a relaxed smile from Gerald who now reduced the anxiety he had created.

"So w*hy* haven't mutant viruses wiped us out? Because they must deliver their payload to the right cell in order to cause disease. Which is too hard for most of them —they need our help to get past their trial-and-error behavior.

"But they can be effective. It took only seven genes for Staphylococcus aureus to make a simple chemistry change in its cell wall, replacing an ester bond with an amide and becoming invulnerable to Vancomycin.

"Think of the process as a computer operation. Seven bacterial species share data causing the single bit alteration necessary to respond to an antibiotic threat. Thankfully, there's usually a trade off between virulence and antibiotic resistance. You don't often get both. Too much information is needed like when your hard drive fills up."

Feeling the need to get back on track, The Major interrupted him.

"We owe Gerald our thanks for his presentation. One which was so clear that even I understood it. But I wonder: can a lethal illness be created which would spread *solely* among women and children?

"A superb question!" Gerald responded, treating it as an invitation to another recitation.

"Think of the American Indians after fifteen hundred. Fifty six million died from the diseases brought by settlers for which they lacked immunity. Not, as is popularly believed, because their immune systems lacked exposure to European microbes but because they lacked *biodiversity*. All were descended from two waves of Asian immigration. Their small gene pool meant that someone's immune response could be easily overcome by new microbes and passed onto another Indian. Thus a virus could become tailor made for these biological relatives.

"A virus lethal only to women and infants requires a germ to hone in on them. Then increase its virulence and decrease resistance factors. This can be tricky since you have to change many genes to also not reduce its viability. You'd need a lab and small scale testing. It could be accomplished in three months with bright enough workers. Five months at most."

"How could you maintain security using outsiders?" asked The Major.

"By dividing the goal into commonplace tasks with only one person seeing everything. Graduate assistants are blinded by concern with their professor's opinion and don't feel the right to question their orders.

"Probably a new strain of TSST-1 would work. To cause physiological chaos in infants with immature immune systems, and their highly stressed mothers. Stress reduces the effectiveness of all human activity."

"Which is why I insist that we take our regular breaks," The Major interjected with a smile. All except Gerald looked relieved. He really enjoys his work, The Major thought, wanting to be alone.

He had expected the project to be completed in five days. Now it would drag on for months, meaning greater risk. His employer was equally naive: eliminating the professors never would have worked. Not for at least five months, until the American holiday of Thanksgiving. But what better time to spread fear than when families relax together?

He had already decided on the target: Manhattan from Chambers Street south to the Battery. New Yorkers living in converted office buildings and lofts. Wealthy men with perfect wives demanding similar babies. How would they respond when both became infected and hospitals filled? Certainly not with resignation. America would hear *their* screams. Which would be even greater now when the World Trade Centers were being re-built and the war against terror was overshadowed by concern with the economy.

The Major was surprised how calm he felt at the prospect of becoming a mass murderer. Though he would be back in Ireland when it began: watching the events on

TV or speaking of them with an elderly priest, both expressing horror.

Forty minutes remained in the break before lunch. He didn't believe that anyone could eat right after Gerald's presentation. They would just wonder what microbes the food might contain. So The Major sat in the club's misnamed Library and again considered his life, now having become increasingly convinced that he need fully understand his motives in order to most effectively manipulate those of others. Though he had spent his years after leaving the Devonmere Correctional Center trying *not* to think, and seeking financial independence which his father had insisted was the only essential goal.

After the success of his initial computer chip theft he avoided direct action, having decided that to plan operations and use intermediaries in exchange for a share of the gains was wisest.

Some months he didn't work. Then he spent his time speaking with his elderly clerical friend, enjoying women, and renovating his house. Blending into the Irish village community even with his atypical health concerns. Like objecting to the tobacco smoke which overhung the pub's ceiling, an eccentricity which his neighbors considered "American." Which he found was true now, during this first trip to America since his childhood. The Major wondered where he really belonged, if anywhere.

But he never questioned this while his father was alive for then he knew that he belonged with him. Now everyone was gone except for a half-sister he barely remembered and a stepmother who had warped his life.

He once read that it took as long to be healed from trauma as the time during which it was experienced. Having been imprisoned in Devonmere for six years perhaps only now was he becoming fully recovered.

Why *had* he taken this risk? The fee significantly increased his assets but he already had far more money than he could ever spend.

He trusted Gerald's judgment with how unwitting graduate assistants were but wondered whether *his* ego would compromise secrecy. Could Gerald *never* speak of his greatest technical achievement? Nor allude to it in an obscure journal article read by unworldly scholars and CIA consultants?

Only now did The Major view this job clearly. His risk was *enormous*. He permitted himself to be flattered by the huge fee, manipulated as easily as were his professors.

Now he remembered another line from the psychology book he read: that people create their fate and unconsciously act to *force themselves* towards a desired change. Did he accept this assignment to climax his career and inaugurate his retirement? Or, from depression, to end his life?

Others entered the Library and a woman smiled at him but The Major didn't notice: he felt paralyzed with horror. There seemed to be no way out! Although he was convinced that the operation would succeed, *must* succeed considering that he had been paid, the Americans would have to discover who did it. Their motivation would be too great to fail. His basic error was that while in the past he had merely created plans, now he was part of another's. Who *was* his employer? Why did they so hate this country?

He remembered the satisfaction which he had gained from aiding the politician son of the Taiwanese manufacturer who had bought his first stolen goods. Then his theft involved the blueprints of the huge underground liquefied natural gas facility at Tuen Mun in Hong Kong's New Territories. This easy prey, which lay in an unguarded shed, was essential to Taiwanese military contingency plans after the takeover of Hong Kong by mainland China. A wise move considering China's recurring threat to invade Taiwan.

To import natural gas economically it must first be liquefied, then reduced to one six hundredth of its vapor volume becoming liquefied natural gas (LNG). Unfortunately this only occurs at minus two hundred sixty degrees Fahrenheit. If released into the atmosphere above sixty degrees a huge explosion results, first flash-freezing and then French-frying everyone in its path. To say nothing of the effect when these heavier than air vapors entered sewers seeking an ignition source.

The energy of the World War Two bombing raid on Tokyo which killed eighty three thousand people was but one hundredth of the force in one of the three LNG tanks at Tuen Mun.

Gaining entry into the shed holding the plans meant merely short-circuiting the alarm cable, then spraying the padlock with liquid nitrogen and shattering it with a hammer blow. He photographed the blueprints, stole small tools to provide the police with evidence of a simple motive, and was back in his hotel by the Shatin railway station in time for breakfast. Which he skipped, anticipating his lunch at its Forget-Me-Not Lounge, a name he inexplicably remembered from a long past trip with his father.

Afterwards, as usual, he tried to forget. But he still periodically remembered how alive he had felt when he approached the shack, a feeling which he lacked since the theft which began his career.

His mind drifted to a Norse proverb which had been told to him by the priest: "Take no vengeance though they do thee wrong." And a Roman one: "Part of us is claimed by our country, part by our parents, part by our friends."

He had, for pay, aided guerrilla organizations and intelligence services. But never in Ireland or Great Britain, wanting his life to remain unhindered. He had no country or caring relatives, except for a priest who possibly considered him the son which he would never have.

Exhausted by these thoughts The Major looked about the room. In a corner was an old fashioned hope chest used by some long ago woman anticipating marriage. He shook his head slightly. So human, unlike his plans for mass murder. Then he remembered advice on the evil of pride, which had been e-mailed to him by the priest.

"Pride causes one to gain pleasure. Not from something, but only because it is not possessed by another. Being continuously competitive is the anti-God state of mind. Why does a beautiful woman collect admirers or a wealthy man greater riches? To be *better than* others. Drunkenness and unchastity bring people together. *Pride* separates them and is the utmost evil. A spiritual cancer which devours common sense."

Now The Major realized that pride, his desire to be *the best,* had overwhelmed his logical thinking. And he sensed that finding a way out required that *he* change. Still, he was convinced that the plan *must* succeed. If not, his life would certainly be ended by his unknown employer, who would not fail.

The Major became calm: a soldier entering battle, his life controlled by fate. As an American president remarked before his assassination, "Life is unfair. You play the cards you were dealt."

He would see how Americans reacted to their hundred thousand deaths.

As the clock chimed he slowly walked towards the conference room, feeling resigned.

The buffet was laid. He nodded at his colleagues, absorbed in their selection. Gerald approached him, shyly, though with a confident smile.

"I'm convinced the plan is doable," he said.

CHAPTER TWENTY TWO

"I DIDN'T NOTICE THIS BEFORE." Heinz referred to the quotation on the cover of the packet which The Major distributed to the participants on their arrival. It came from a report on biological warfare which had been prepared for the Secretary of War after America entered World War Two.

"Any method advantageous to a nation at war will be vigorously employed. There is but one logical course. To study such warfare from every angle, making every preparation to reduce its effectiveness and the likelihood of its use."

The mood was subdued, all being affected by the seriousness of their task. Gerald's presentation made real what had seemed theoretical. Democratic institutions laid siege by narco-terrorists, and others who feared the uncertainty of freedom and pain of autonomy.

The scholars went to war: to defend their families, and civilization.

A day earlier The Major would have been pleased. Now he remembered a movie which had been shown at Devonmere by the soccer coach who sought to rally his prisoner/players. A football classic with its famous line, "One more for The Gipper." Now, feeling momentarily aroused, The Major felt better until his feeling of depression returned. Which he had expected for he knew that depression naturally occurred when one became frozen by terrifying alternatives.

Gerald noted The Major's change of expression.

"Don't look so sad. You hired the right people. Your plan'll knock 'em dead."

All laughed and the atmosphere lightened. Then, with the food plates cleared, the scholars continued their struggle to protect freedom.

"We need a time plan, itemization of staff and equipment, and estimates of cost and casualties." The Major said.

"Our bureaucrat," Calvin jibed. All smiled, then again became solemn.

"Three hundred fifty thousand dollars," said Gerald.

"Under a hundred million isn't serious money in Washington," Calvin interjected.

"Three hundred eighty thousand," Gerald corrected after scribbling on a pad. "Possibly twenty percent higher."

"Staff? Equipment? Potential casualties?" The Major asked.

"A microbiologist and engineer. The viral agent would be grown in fertilized hens' eggs. You'd need a bottling plant with sterilization capacity," itemized Gerald.

"Also a dispersal device and plan of attack," added Calvin.

Gerald resumed speaking. "Casualties would be approximately one hundred forty thousand with ninety seven percent mortality, ninety percent of these being mothers or infants. The rest, those who were immunologically impaired: suffering from AIDS or some type of cancer."

"What protection will be needed for the staff?" The Major didn't want a publicized accident.

"Just surgical gloves and mask."

"Dispersal device?"

Calvin spoke. "You'd want the virus spread within a particular area. A slurry on subway walls with the spores spreading as it dried would work, but this method would contaminate the rest of the city." He thought quietly for a moment. "No. What would be best is a van spreading the germ through a phony exhaust pipe over lower Manhattan on Sunday morning. When mostly only residents would be about."

"When could the plan could be placed into operation?" asked The Major.

"Three months tops would be needed for a field tested study," Gerald answered, to general agreement. "You'd need another seventy thousand dollars for the modified van."

"Without leather seats!" The Major insisted, forcing a grin which the others readily joined.

"It's standard in the model."

"OK, but definitely no video player," The Major added with a wry smile. As if knowing that he was being taken advantage of but accepting it. A pose which inspired loyalty, his father had once said.

Little work now remained except to write a detailed schematic and to name it. Calling it "The Plan" no longer sufficed. Not for the imaginary generals and bureaucrats, or his employer who might want to publicize it. Their correspondence had been pedantic: an exchange between gentlemen who understood the gravity of failure.

The scholars bantered, being unwilling to leave the comfort of companionship for their room's isolation. So The Major tried woolgathering.

"What can we name the plan?"

"Something dramatic to demand attention," Calvin began. "Maybe with a biological implication since it involves a C/B weapon," Gerald added."

"No," Heinz added firmly, "a different tone. Let me tell you a story."

All sprawled in their chairs, loving good ones.

"Who was the most important Soviet defector?" he asked, implying that his question was rhetorical.

"Yurchenko," his colleagues said simultaneously, playing along.

"Not even if his re-defection was honest. I'd say Sejna."

The Major spoke for them: "He was Czech."

"Just beginning my story," Heinz said, unfazed by the correction. "He was the highest ranking defector in the decision process. He knew of the Soviet plan to invade Switzerland in time of war, turn Cuba into a revolutionary center, and to use Eastern Bloc chemical and biological weapons.

"The Soviets never considered these weapons to be inferior to nuclear bombs. From their point of view each could substitute for the other. Knowing how distasteful Western nations considered C/B use, they only pretended to abide by the Geneva treaty against them. So they would speak of 'special weapons' and use the code words BUTTERFLY and SPRUCE. In the nineteen sixties their research went into high gear to be able to defeat potential enemies like China. Its massive territory and huge population made it invulnerable to nuclear assault. Using C/B could 'make them sleep forever.' And defeat Western Europe without destroying its industry.

"Our plan describes the possible doom of humanity. Thus it should be named: Operation *CATACLYSM*."

All were impressed by Heinz' fervor. To foster camaraderie, The Major suggested that a vote be taken and the title was unanimously approved.

Then, with one day remaining, the scholars adjourned for the evening having a sense of great accomplishment.

CHAPTER TWENTY THREE

THE FINAL MEETING began early. The scholars, being eager to share their conclusions and leave, spoke little while eating breakfast.

With just coffee, fruit, and pastries remaining on the sideboard, The Major structured their presentations. First, Gerald would summarize information about the germ's production, and the likely medical response to its activation. Then Calvin would describe its dissemination and the terrorists' escape plan. Heinz would conclude by assessing the political and military reactions to the crisis.

"Why am I first?" Gerald asked with feigned annoyance. He loved an audience and his rhetorical question met with knowing smiles as The Major set the tone of their discussion.

"Your critical attitudes can produce shattering insights. While not wanting to discourage these I emphasize that we're colleagues giving emotional support, not slash-to-the-jugular academicians. Save this attitude for the terrorists."

Following this priming, Gerald put down his coffee and began speaking.

"I'm glad that we're through," he said, glaring at Heinz. Who hastily gobbled his cheese Danish, then sprawled with pen and pad balanced atop his stomach.

"Within the first hour of Operation CATACLYSM, or C plus one Sunday morning, for which name we're greatly indebted to Heinz (he nodded towards him), most women, infants, and immune-deficient older individuals of both sexes living in New York City south of Chambers Street will begin their painful journey towards death.

"What symptoms develop will depend on the specific agent cloned. Its ability to be tailored to particular populations can no longer be questioned: the Epstein-Barr virus gives whites a relatively harmless ailment, the notorious 'kissing disease' of mononucleosis, yet causes Africans and Southeast Asians to develop *two* types of cancer.

"The presenting symptoms may include fever above a hundred two Fahrenheit, vomiting, diarrhea, low blood pressure and difficulty breathing, coughing up blood, dizziness when standing.

"A rash looking like sunburn may not develop until the late stage, and then on only a small area and not be noticed. Pain in the groin. Some will have aching muscles or a sore throat making it seem like the flu.

"The initial response will be...puzzlement. For the symptoms will resemble toxic shock syndrome toxin-1, TSST-1, but differ. The first cases which reach hospitals will use up all of the available antibiotics: penicillin, the cephalosporin families comprising the betalactam antibiotics. Even the most potent drug, Vancomycin, will fail. Patients will deteriorate and emergency rooms will be overwhelmed. Many doctors today are women and most who are living in the infected area will be dying.

"There will be much activity but little effect. Misdiagnoses will abound. Some will be considered suffering from anxiety. Detectors being developed by DARPA* can instantly pick out volatile molecules released by damaged lung membranes indicating biological attack, but none are in use.

"To summarize: doctors and the public will panic. Ever since the Middle Ages infectious agents have been the greatest source of terror.

"Production of the microbe would be simple. We've been able to grow mammalian cells on the surface of minute beads. The introduction of continuous flow fermentors and hollow fiber technology has permitted a hundred fold reduction in the time and material necessary. It can be done. Definitely."

Gerald reached for his coffee and smiled at the brief applause. All had been impressed.

The Major nodded towards Calvin who, after clearing his throat, began speaking.

"First, the dissemination. A computer grid would

*Defense Advanced Research Projects Agency

be prepared of streets in the target area. The van would travel along each while spewing the germ through its phony exhaust pipe. This method was validated by Iraq.

"Two passes would be made for maximum dispersion although one should suffice. The agent could be placed in large micro capsules containing smaller ones having different time release rates. This makes it less hazardous to the terrorists, aids viability of the virus, and insures sustained contamination of the area.

"The terrorists will wear respirators, gloves, and clothing impregnated with N-halamines—chlorine compounds which effectively kill the virus after contact. Their escape will present no greater difficulty than for other unknown criminals. They may choose to flee the country or just the city. Depending on when the micro capsules are release—I would recommend six o'clock when residents start being up and about—the terrorists should be perfectly safe by the time the virus becomes operative. But they may leave quickly, not sharing confidence in our methodology."

All enjoyed Calvin's understated joke, then looked expectantly towards Heinz. Bored after years of anonymous academic struggle they yearned to effect public life: pontificate on *The Larry King Show* or be interviewed by Barbara Walters. What *would be* the impact of their work?

"We know a little from the World Trade Centers' horror: a devastating effect will occur," he summarized.

"The patient count will quickly overwhelm hospitals.

Wealthy residents who control America's financial infrastructure—major political donors—will demand nonexistent medical services.

"Eventually someone will conclude that a biological agent was activated. NEST's* Blue Team will arrive but fail to isolate this virus with its flu-like symptoms which are resistant to antibiotics. The mortality rate will be similar to cholera but Vibrio cholerae will be absent from stool samples. Finally they'll conclude that a manufactured bug is responsible. Maybe (he nodded towards Gerald) one engineered to grow at other than the usual temperature and medium. Or not until it combines with milk lactose and reaches the small intestine. So those using milk would be most affected by it."

"Ingenious," Gerald interjected, with an almost affectionate grin.

"The political reaction will match the panic of civilians. A Top Event never expected and prayed against has occurred. With no possible treatment, funeral pyres will light South Street Seaport. American self-confidence will crumble."

"What would be the military reaction?" The Major asked.

*A counterpart organization of the Nuclear Emergency Search Teams designated to deal with threats of a biological or chemical nature.

"Martial law will be declared with much aimless activity. Soldiers are trained to kill but who? What will be the next target? Missiles will be unfurled but against which nation? Doctors will flee, and sailors avoid shore leave."

This attempt at humor failed for his presentation had been too graphic.

Though still depressed, The Major was pleased with his creation. Operation *CATACLYSM* would elate his employer. Yet, knowing of plans becoming bungled through poor luck, accident, karma, or call it what you will, he feared that an unforeseen element could sabotage it, and cause his life to end even more quickly than now seemed likely.

"I congratulate you. Civilized nations will be in your debt. But before leaving for your well earned relaxation, I'd like consideration of possible interdictions. Could we have missed something?"

The scholars pondered, annoyed that their expertise was being questioned by a layman although conceding the matter's importance.

Gerald posed several. "The van may be stopped by police who wonder at its low speed and why it follows no apparent destination. The driver may talk after escaping from germ infested lower Manhattan but before all of the micro capsules have discharged their contents."

"Solutions?" The Major asked.

Calvin had anticipated these concerns.

"The van will have Federal Environmental

Protection Agency markings and allegedly be monitoring air quality by checking for pollution from coal firing plants in the Midwest. A colored pipe will stick out from a window: for *sample collection.* Its lethal discharge is invisible and won't be noticed.

The escape plan will be smeared with a RICIN*/DMSO mixture. DMSO relieves the pain of arthritis but is a wonderful transmittal agent, speeding the effect of RICIN which kills with such different symptoms: convulsions, stupor, vomiting, bloody diarrhea. This will confuse medical investigators and provide an added benefit: the terrorists would be eliminated so their capture need no longer be feared."

"Anything else?" The Major asked, thinking that if his bloodthirsty scholars were typical of academia then the military might best be trained on campuses—to which locations such impregnated letters could be mailed.

No one spoke. All were anxious to be on their way. Then The Major asked a question which he had wondered about since the previous evening.

"How soon can the devastation be ended if the terrorists' demands are met?"

*RICIN: A poison easily made from Castor beans and a thousand times more toxic than the most advanced nerve agents.

The three looked stunned: like children who had been ordered to surrender water guns which they painstakingly loaded. Gerald spoke for them all.

"The virus will die naturally but only after the death of its hosts: all of the women and infants in lower Manhattan."

CHAPTER TWENTY FOUR

ALL OF HIS CONSULTANTS would be gone by nine. The Major had arranged their final dinner carefully, wanting it to be festive yet serious in tone. While his task was over, theirs had just begun: a tested virus and operational plan were needed within four months. For which added activity each would receive a bonus of four hundred thousand dollars.

A surprise for their creativity they would be told. Actually, it was to insure the plan's completion and their silence. *One* payment for *one* involvement the authorities *might* consider to reflect their naiveté, but *two*?

The date for the operation was suggested by his employer who believed that, occurring then, it would most effectively depress American morale. But he wanted a professional opinion which his *Society of Scholars*, as he had begun to think of them, could provide.

They arrived at six, with packed bags and ready to depart as anonymously as they had arrived.

Despite small talk, all awaited The Major's words.

"Your notes support viability of the plan which, if made public, will be credited to you, I remaining unknown.

"What is missing are a detailed timetable and the tested virus. These are due fourteen weeks from today, with notice of completion sent to the Liechtenstein address."

An angry murmur arose for the scholars had considered their work to be completed.

Anticipating this, The Major raised his hand for silence, then resumed speaking.

"I recognize that you've already earned your fee and the remainder was wired to your accounts today. Upon receipt of the final materials you'll each receive a bonus of four hundred thousand dollars."

Smiles replaced frowns, but one matter remained to be decided.

"We haven't yet determined the most favorable day to conduct such an operation," The Major began. "As you know, terrorism is intended not to physically destroy the enemy but to disrupt its military or political functioning at low cost. Your fees wouldn't buy one armed helicopter. So, on what date would this action paralyze America?"

"Over Christmas weekend," Gerald suggested, "when Americans are relaxed."

"On New Year's Day," offered Heinz, "since the action impacts on the nation's future."

Perhaps his employer was wrong, The Major thought. Then Calvin spoke.

"No," he said in a surprisingly loud voice. "On only one day do Americans remember their origin: fleeing

European tyranny, and the fullness of their bounty. A day which no other nation shares."

Since Calvin was the only American present, The Major wondered at his employers' nationality since they drew the same conclusion.

"The Sunday of Thanksgiving weekend," he insisted.

CHAPTER TWENTY FIVE

CURIOSITY AND BOREDOM had caused Dalling to accept Tower's proposal. Plus the money. Even *two* pensions weren't enough to pay the exorbitant school taxes in Stone Ridge where New York City émigrés and childless models demanded ever smaller classes.

Like many he had wondered about Beekman. Particularly after his comment that "people are moved by love and fear and the knack is finding the right proportion." And Beekman's tendency to argue extravagantly for everything which aroused doubt that he really believed in anything except himself. No one doubted that. Or that he was a formidable bastard.

But why was Tower so worried? Little things wouldn't bother him. If just a quarter of the rumors were true he had gotten half of Congress out of trouble since he arrived in Washington in the nineteen sixties. Nixon's distrust of him, perhaps caused by his overwhelming paranoia about strangers, may even be why he had never asked Tower for help and Watergate happened. Or perhaps Tower was then too busy lobbying for tax changes to help the Beekman family's interests—which then didn't yet include Ralph's political goals.

Dalling agreed that the risk was minimal even if the outcome of any crime wasn't certain. He remembered what happened when President Carter discovered *two* counterinsurgency units when only one was authorized: nothing. Just abandoning one and Pentagon muttering that the "snake-eaters are out of control again." This, after tens of millions of dollars were spent and nonsensical rumors abounded of a military coup in America of all places.

So how dangerous was it? Audio recording *was* illegal and an embarrassing public hearing might result. But Dalling smiled as he imagined lawyers attacking two befuddled senior citizens before TV cameras (him and Tower). And the demonstration which Tower would arrange by irate fellow AARP members. The investigators would be the laughingstock of the country and Beekman would get more votes though he would sense the truth.

After spending several days in Omaha with his grandson to clear his mind, Dalling began to earn Tower's fifty thousand dollar advance by producing the assignment's cover. Downloading, printing, and collating information from the Defense Technical Information Center at Ft. Belvoir and the Strategic and Defense Studies Centre of the Australian National University. More from the U. S. Army's War College Conference on the recent Russian election. Then he bound these pages into a large blue folder he entitled, "Issues and Influences On Political-Military Relations In Transition." Impressive.

Tower had given him a blueprint of the apartment, its keys, Beekman's weekly schedule, and carte blanche.

Dalling initially believed that audio recording would suffice. Then he concluded that it was likely Tower wouldn't be able to recognize all of the voices even with his hearing aid and this decided the matter.

He placed audio bugs in each room's phone, and audio and video transmitters in the temperature controls, wall clock in the kitchen, and stereo speaker in the living room. To bug the emergency light opposite the apartment's entrance would be overkill, he concluded. The receivers would be concealed behind a false panel in the kitchen's utility closet with the audio/video feeds retrieved weekly.

Tower planned to introduce him to the doorman as a researcher who would occasionally use the quiet apartment for writing. Which meant that he could also charge a laptop to his expenses.

He stopped at eleven to watch the late news: stories of the usual fire, robbery, and another ambiguous police shooting. Finally a statement by Beekman about the angry resignation of one of his aides, who had termed his management style "madness." "I'd call it controlled chaos and creative tension: the only way to produce solutions in this entrenched bureaucracy we call government. Just one person in my office was given power and responsibility by the people: me.

The interviewer seemed impressed. So was Dalling.

CHAPTER TWENTY SIX

IT'S OVER, THE MAJOR thought, as he packed his clothes. He had initially requested five days of his scholars' time but had reserved the rooms for an additional week. And would have used it if necessary, hinting that their fees were yet to be paid. "Motivation comes from within. The best worker *wants* to do what you hire them for," his father once said, adding in a later lesson that "money helps."

But his scholars were gone, having wanted to do what he needed. And for the money.

Which left him with a free day. He would have liked to buy gifts but maintained contact with none of his relatives and wouldn't further deceive his current lover with presents.

Then he thought of the former colleague who had advised him by e-mail how much friendlier it was in the Bahamas. A former security guard at the Nuclear-Biological-Chemical defense facility of the German Federal Armed Forces outside Kiel, he had been introduced by The Major to a Taiwanese politician, who warmly welcomed him. Following research into environmental systems, West German naval ships had become impregnable to chemical or biological assault, as did the newer craft of Taiwan. The generous payment for information made possible his friend's very early retirement.

But this man lacked nothing. Then The Major thought of his clerical friend. Who would better appreciate an expensive gift than one enduring poverty?

Pleased with his conclusion he left the club and, walking slowly, peered into stores on Madison Avenue. He considered the purchase of a cashmere coat until doubting its fitness with the priest's other, modest clothes. Then a telescope, remembering his enjoyment at viewing the sea and his quote of the Roman saying that "to live according to nature is the supreme good."

So he bought for him a replica of Admiral Nelson's hand held telescope and a leather bound copy of Montaigne's essays. Then he walked towards Central Park.

He entered at its Fifty-ninth Street entrance and kept himself from trying the telescope only by remembering his need to avoid attracting notice. So instead, he watched the ducks in the lake and women pushing strollers. One seated herself beside him and asked the time. An au pair, she too came from England— Grimsby. Both had watched the local football team, the Mariners, play at Blundell Park. Suddenly he looked at his watch, referred to an appointment and left. Then, wondering at his abruptness, he concluded that she was about to ask a personal question and the difficulty which this presented for one who led his unusual life.

Now, again feeling depressed, he remembered the

address of his half-sister. Without further thought, he walked quickly to Grand Central Station. There, he bought coffee, a bagel, and a newspaper. Just like a typical commuter waiting for the next train. He felt better at having a goal.

The Major had learned of his stepmother's remarriage while he was at Devonmere. Her later childbirth gave him distant relatives who lacked interest for him. But he and his sister *were* of the same blood, and he wondered which parent she resembled.

At the Scarsdale train station he rented a car and drove to their house. Though driven by curiosity, he knew that to enter would be foolish, creating unanswerable questions and even possible police involvement. So he sat in his car while awaiting a glimpse of his sister, Letitia. An odd name he believed, until being informed by his priestly friend that it derived from Latin and meant gladness.

An investigator once advised him about conducting surveillance from a car: to sit in the passenger seat and, while apparently waiting for the driver's return, face away from the house using the side and rear view mirrors for observation. But he ignored this suggestion, relying instead on the heavily tinted windows which made use of his newly purchased telescope possible.

At three fifteen a tall teenage girl parked in the driveway and walked from her car. She demanded that the two children in hand, "stop it now!" He thought of striking up a conversation but knew how suspicious Americans were of strangers. So he finished his coffee, being thankful for his bladder's sake that it was decaffeinated.

A half hour later the girl left the house and stood briefly on the porch. He felt she sensed he was there even as he knew that this thought was nonsense. Then he noted their resemblance: both were tall and fair with an angular facial structure. Like so many others.

He followed as she drove to a Media Play store. She briefly disappeared in back. Then she reappeared wearing a blue sales jacket and walked towards the computer behind a counter. Holding a Diet Coke he had purchased from a cooler, The Major strolled the aisles and watched her interact with customers. Her boredom was evident and, considering her family's prosperity, he wondered why she worked. Once, sensing his attention, she glanced briefly at him.

Now for the second time that day and only the third time in his life The Major behaved impulsively. He walked towards the woman who might be his sister.

After entering Devonmere he had long imagined them playing like children again. Now he confronted a grown near-woman and wondered what to say. So he played it by ear.

"Can I help?" she asked. He considered her speech faintly accented but knew that its lack of accent wouldn't evidence anything. Letitia had left England when she was four and might have lost it. The name tag read "Angela" but he knew that many clerks used pseudonyms to protect themselves.

The Major smiled. She didn't respond and he wondered what caused her to be so suspicious at her young age. Suddenly he thought of a book he once found at Devonmere: the autobiography of a German communist which described his intrigues, capture and torture by the Nazis, and eventual flight to America. Identifying with the author, The Major had read it frequently until his release.

"I wonder if a book is available. *Out Of The Night* by Jan Valtin. His real name is Richard Krebs."

Now the girl-woman smiled, no longer feeling uneasy that he was trying to pick her up.

"I'll check." She turned and typed the title into the computer. Nothing came up. "I'll try another," she said, now using the author's names. "Maybe it'll be on the Web." Then, "It's *really* old. A nineteen forty one Book-Of-The-Month Club selection." She printed the review which both read.

"I can see why you want it. Maybe an out-of-print book site'll have it. I'll try Bibliofind.com, then Bookfinder.com. They waited. "The computer's slow," she explained.

"British?" she asked.

"Yes." Though traveling on a phony Irish passport.

"You have the same accent as in the thirties' movies my friend loves."

"Any in particular?"

"Things To Come."

"Destroying the world to create a better one," he said. Which was, possibly, his employer's motive.

The words startled her and he wondered if she shared this desire, then concluded it likely that all adolescents did.

"Where do you live?" she asked.

"London." A safe lie.

"What's it like?"

"Masses of people, increasingly American. You'd feel at home."

"I'm British," she said.

Now The Major felt startled. He expected having to fit bits of information towards a conclusion, not gain immediate certainty. To conceal his surprise he took a sip from his drink.

"*Really.*"

"Dual citizenship. Born in England. I was here since I was four."

The Major sipped more. "Angela?"

She shook her head. "LeeAnn."

Letitia, he thought. His stepmother's attempt to erase the past.

A novel warmth pervaded The Major as he harshly rejected another impulse of this surprising day: to reveal his identity and embrace her. The computer screen came alive.

"Bibliofind has three copies in different conditions. Eighteen, fifteen, and eleven dollars. Should I order one?"

"How long will delivery take?" he asked, needing an excuse.

"Two to three days."

"Better not. I'm leaving tomorrow."

"Going home."

Home, to a building where he just worked and slept.

He stood silently, being unwilling to leave yet unable to think of how to extend their contact. He felt certain that she would reject his invitation for coffee/tea/soda. So he smiled again, "You've been very helpful."

"English courtesy," she said impishly.

He gave a knowing grin and left quickly before blurting out what he hungered to say: You need never be afraid. We shared the same father and all I have is yours."

CHAPTER TWENTY SEVEN

LeeAnn's stomach was bigger and sucking it in didn't work anymore. Not that she did it often. Just when she was expecting an embarrassing question from someone after they began looking puzzled.

It was her sixth month and she knew that she better tell. Valerie was pressuring her and Ralph was cleverer than he knew when he kissed her "baby fat." Wonder if he'll feel the same about its cause, LeeAnn thought, and felt more frightened than ever.

She had always been alone, needing to care for herself, The Monsters, even her parents. Which she learned wasn't unusual for the children of alcoholics in the one Al-A-Teen meeting she attended. But that group wasn't for her. Teenagers gossiped, and she didn't need any more people advising her to have an abortion.

Two months earlier she took three hundred dollars from her stepfather's wallet and drove to an abortion clinic in Yonkers. Then she fled with the completed intake form and her final decision: to keep the baby, and attend an expectant mothers class. Which were full even in Westchester County, where many pregnant students were offered expensive vacations by their parents from which they returned noticeably slimmer.

LeeAnn considered running away but she couldn't leave The Monsters with her alcoholic parents. Maybe in ten years it would be OK but not now. So she was stuck in Scarsdale, and vowed to tell Ralph about her pregnancy—*their baby*—tonight.

When would be the best time to tell? In the shower? After they had sex? During breakfast? Finally she decided that the best time would be when it felt right. She was hopeful that she wouldn't blurt it out. She would be calm. Just like she was when she refused his offer of cocaine, though agreeing that she needed to relax. Ralph then complimented her on her "virtue" without sarcasm. Which was another reason why she loved him and blamed only herself for her situation.

Despite all of the boys who had wanted inside her virginal pants, she chose someone old enough to be her father. Maybe Valerie was right in saying that she was looking for a father, her stepfather having been only a good provider. Both he *and* her biological father were wealthy. LeeAnn could trust her mother for this.

These thoughts went through LeeAnn's mind on Friday, after she awoke from a nightmare in which a car which she was driving went increasingly out of control. Just like her life, she realized.

The previous day she had acted on Valerie's information about pregnancy causing plaque buildup and saw a dentist. She was nervous as he cleaned her teeth, and he tried to relax her by chattering about the Wu Tang Clan band and Dr. Groove HotWatch his daughter liked. As if all teenagers were the same, she thought.

But her earlier nausea didn't appear and she stopped carrying the crackers which David had advised, sometimes wishing that he were her lover. Then she reminded herself that she didn't really know him, thought of Valerie, and felt guilty.

The alarm went off, meaning that she had a half hour to shower and dress before getting The Monsters up. Upon standing she felt a sharp pain in her stomach. So she got back into bed and closed her eyes, imagining herself lying on a warm beach as David had advised. Soon the pain went away but this, and persistent headaches or vaginal bleeding, were symptoms he had warned her about. She would tell him tonight. Another worry.

Thankfully, the morning was peaceful. After that first weekend The Monsters loved staying with Aunt Valerie and Uncle David, and his cat which they took turns cradling. Threatening their weekly visit became more effective than refusing sweets at keeping them in line.

School went OK until a girl said that if LeeAnn kept putting on weight she would be going to the tenth grade prom alone. Which was now as elaborate as the Seniors' prom, complete with its limousine transportation and morning after breakfast at a hotel.

She must have looked gloomy because David spent more time talking with her than usual. He diagnosed her pain that morning as being gas and advised her again about a healthy diet. And to see an obstetrician, though he didn't know one who would treat her without her parents being involved. "I'm your friend, not your doctor," he insisted. She didn't argue, being thankful for his help and knowing that doctors could be sued even for giving free advice.

"Don't worry," he cautioned, but didn't tell her how not to. Just like most doctors.

LeeAnn delayed leaving the loft, playing with The Monsters and even the cat, until Valerie looked at her quizzically. She didn't want to stay, just not to leave.

While driving to Beekman Place she absentmindedly blocked an intersection. Then she avoided getting a ticket by hiking her skirt, crying, and giving her phone number to the policeman. Being only sixteen she wasn't allowed to drive in New York City and couldn't risk having to call her parents for help on today of all days.

After parking, she remembered having forgotten to buy the whole grain bread and salad dressing which Ralph liked but she felt too tired to get back into the car. She was driving everywhere these days.

Ralph didn't make telling easy. Sprawled on the sofa with reading glasses perched down his nose, he waved her towards him, moving a stack of documents from his side of the sofa to the floor. Several were bordered in red and stamped "SECRET." Without thinking, she remarked, "secret, just like our love." These words led to their first fight.

Ralph frowned. "Are you tired?"

She was but didn't tell him why, being unsure that now was the right moment.

"Of sneaking and worrying."

Ralph considered her tone to be different than usual, more adult-like. As if she were his wife, which he had again fantasized that day.

"I hate it too. Being with my wife and wanting you. Watching the kind of mother she is and how you care for your sisters. I know you brought them up, and what your mother is really like." He suppressed a grin at the thought of how well he knew her mother.

Then he looked hurt and sad and LeeAnn snuggled against him, desperate for warmth and hating herself for it.

Minutes later, calmer, she nodded towards the folders. "Should they be here?"

"Technically no, but where else can a senator think clearly. The president asked me to come over last night and we talked till three. That's why I need you. Others know only part of me, you know everything."

Except how to tell him that I'm pregnant, LeeAnn thought. She cooked for him while he read, being his emotional support while he changed America, Ralph thought. But he decided to hold that line for another day and felt slightly ashamed at how effectively he had manipulated her. Because he loved her.

Later, after showering alone like a typical wife, LeeAnn put on the nightgown she had surreptitiously borrowed from her mother. But she quickly took it off, fearing that it made her look pregnant. Instead, she wore one of the unisex bathrobes hanging behind the bathroom door as she got into bed with Ralph.

Who was still reading. LeeAnn had never seen him so serious and wondered what else she didn't know about him.

She watched the TV news using headphones, preferring a movie but wanting to seem grown-up. Soon Ralph put his papers on the floor, reached under the covers and fondled her. This had always excited her but now she felt that she would rather watch TV and wondered what had changed: being pregnant, or something in their relationship.

But having sex was easier than thinking and both soon felt so much that Ralph said he loved her and she whispered the same. Then, before falling asleep, she wondered what their words really meant.

Telling him happened unexpectedly the next morning. Ralph was reading in the living room and, as she passed, he said softly, "You look pregnant."

LeeAnn blurted, "I am."

Everything stopped. His reading. Her thinking. Maybe the clock too.

"You're joking."

LeeAnn wanted to agree but knew that if she lied she would never be able to tell him.

"Sixth month."

He motioned her towards him and they embraced like twelve hours before, though now so much was different.

CHAPTER TWENTY EIGHT

THEY LOOKED YOUNGER than their years but no longer felt uncomfortable when compensating for their ages. So, following the walk suggested by Dalling and abbreviated by Tower, they ate on the patio and listened to Dalling's recordings, before burning them with the garbage. Tower felt comforted by his friend's laconic communication, it reminding him of his Midwestern roots.

"Pretty," Dalling remarked looking at LeeAnn's photo. "Young too."

"Hopefully never younger. Was it hard to find out?"

"They're rarely seen together. She could be visiting another apartment. The doorman is Finnish and acts like he just came over so unless a reporter speaks it..."

"And paid better."

"That too."

They paused to finish the ham they bought during their walk. Dalling liked living close to town. This had reduced his wife's sense of isolation during her final months. Now he chatted with famous models at the supermarket and was back doing surveillance, an odd combination for his retirement years.

Tower noticed Dalling's change of mood and surmised correctly that he had been thinking of his wife. So he quickly began speaking of business matters, believing that this would be best for Dalling, which was true. Beekman's father was a master manipulator who had long instructed Tower in this art, which he then taught to Ralph.

"How far pregnant is she?" Tower asked.

"She said her sixth month though at her age she could be off."

"You'd think that he would have been more careful," Tower said wearily.

"You mean the pregnancy *wasn't* deliberate?"

Tower smiled. Beekman's sexual impulsiveness was now widely known.

"What now?" Dalling asked.

"We listen, and wait."

"Do her parents know she's pregnant?"

Tower was sure that they didn't for LeeAnn's betrayed mother had not yet having appeared on *Good Morning America*. But he wouldn't tell Dalling this and hoped that he would never find out what his senator was capable of.

"Probably not. LeeAnn would have told him."

Having parented teenage girls, Dalling didn't think Tower was right, but he had learned from his years in the military never to question a boss' firmly held conclusion.

"Want to see the movies?"

"Just her still photo."

Tower found private knowledge distasteful and remembered a story about JFK, when he was caught in a hotel with a prostitute. After the manager asserted that he had a woman with him, JFK insisted she was his secretary and that he didn't like being disturbed. Then the manager called again. "Senator, I apologize for intruding but security says your secretary is well known along Pennsylvania Avenue as being a prostitute. I tell you this for the sake of your reputation." "A notorious woman," JFK responded, "How shocking. I'll fire her in the morning."

Tower preferred Lincoln's attitude. When seeing a colleague with a prostitute, he remarked "the fellow looked conscious of his guilt." But that was in another century.

Tower studied LeeAnn's picture. She was a beautiful girl, one who he sensed that he knew though not from among his few young acquaintances. Then he faintly recalled a long past diplomatic reception. Perhaps she resembled... "Do you have her mother's photo?"

Dalling rummaged through a file folder and, from it, picked one of a Westchester fund raising breakfast. He pointed to a striking, thirtyish woman. "Probably older than she looks."

LeeAnn looks nothing like her, Tower thought. "Which is her father?"

"Her *stepfather* is arm-in-arm with Beekman," Dalling said, barely concealing his distaste. Her father is dead. She's adopted."

"He must have died young. Military?"

"I don't know. He was English."

Tower felt annoyed. He was anxious but not about the quality of Dalling's work. For Ralph to bed mother and daughter was bad enough but for LeeAnn to have a dead diplomat or military hero for her father would be disastrous.

"Find out what you can about him. Anything else I should know?"

"Another felony. He takes classified files home."

"So do most senators. He could be thrown off the Intelligence Committee for it. More likely that he would be applauded for his Puritan ethic after he finished defending himself. No more at our first brunch I hope."

Now Dalling became cautious. Older lawyers than Tower had become scandalized.

"Who pays Beekman's bills?"

"Me."

"All of them?"

"Tell me." Tower said impatiently.

"A wire transfer in the millions from the Craxton Diamond Company to a Geneva account. The recorder blurred and I don't have a technician to clear it."

"When?"

"It was referred to on the first day the equipment was operating."

Tower considered but then rejected having Dalling investigate further. Flagging it would increase the likelihood it became public though he doubted it involved anything fraudulent. Like most of the super-wealthy, Beekman didn't pay attention to money. He never carried any, having others pay his bills and be reimbursed later.

But a sum in the millions involved a major undertaking even for him. Which bothered Tower. Not out of pique at information being kept from him, but because he knew how Beekman acted. He tended to hold firmly to beliefs and bulldoze ahead even when he was hopelessly wrong. Which was part of the personality makeup of a political genius, but could produce disasters.

"What does Craxton sell?" Tower asked.

"Not jewelry uncut gems. They're easily transported but selling that large an amount disrupts the market and takes time. They probably insisted on a wire transfer to verify that the money wasn't being laundered."

Now Tower wished he lived in the last century: there was no Lincoln here. Not wanting Dalling to sense his distress he changed the subject.

"He has a business mind like his father. He's laying the seeds for another fortune. Or harem."

Dalling smiled, but wondered what Beekman had said before the bugs were in place.

CHAPTER TWENTY NINE

THE MAJOR KNEW that nothing could be changed and so he passed his days typically. Being up at five which, since his incarceration at Devonmere, had structured his biological clock. Then breakfasting on sardines, tomato, bread, and coffee before his walk along barely charted roads, where he sometimes chatted with a horse riding pre-adolescent before they parted at the fork towards Drogheda. Once he was stopped by two unkempt men demanding to know whether he was Catholic or Protestant. Uncertain of their sobriety or sanity, he grasped the 9mm Walther in his jacket and replied that he sympathized with all men who wished to live freely. His cryptic answer was apparently good enough for they left him in peace.

But his elderly clerical friend took the incident seriously, reminding him that he should remember how closely he lived to a border where the wrong word might cost his life. Now The Major felt that rage which he experienced when anyone tried to abridge his freedom, but tended to interfere with sound behavior. "No," he said, "they were never closer to death."

The priest stared and then turned away. He had learned of The Major's capacities at their first meeting. Outside a Dublin bookstore where he was reading unaffordable editions of the medieval philosophers he loved.

Waiting after dark at a desolate corner for the last bus to Dundalk, wearing civilian clothes and not appearing to be a priest, several men tried to rob him. A passerby saw what was happening and stopped. Viewing *his* greater prosperity the men approached him. After glancing hesitantly, their prey ran. They pursued him, cries rang out, then...silence.

The priest feared that the stranger had become victim in his place. But moments later the man left the alley, straightened his clothes, and offered a lift. As they talked in the car, the cleric revealed his calling and concern. The man smiled. "The Lord protects the guardians of His sheep," he said.

Next day the priest scanned the Dublin newspaper. Four men had suffered broken bones and abrasions; three would be hospitalized for months, one walking forever with a limp. A knife, iron pipe, and revolver were found, belonging, they said, to the Belfast Provos who attacked them. Despite their serious injuries the article's tone implied that few would believe them. Likely they were drunk and had fought.

Though they lived in the same village, the priest had never previously spoken with this man who others termed "The Major." A nickname he too began using though he doubted that it derived from soldiering for the man's clothes were too expensive and his bearing was too relaxed.

Also, he treated everyone, from street sweeper to judge, the same. All liked him though none knew him well. Not even the woman who confessed to the priest their sin, which was merely a less common sexual practice.

Soon they began sharing a table at the local pub and alternating dinners at their homes. His housekeeper, scathing even with him, nurtured The Major. "Can't you see that he never had a mother?" she asked. The priest couldn't, and concluded that this reflected another of his inadequacies.

Years passed and they became closer. The priest revealed that it was his discomfort with clerical politics which had prevented him from achieving higher rank, while The Major spoke of impersonal matters: renovations to his house and local events. Periodically he would leave unannounced for weeks, sometimes returning tanned. A change from his usual pale complexion for he walked outdoors only at dawn and kept his windows shuttered.

His being the only house with air-conditioning, some considered him foppish. But the priest sensed that The Major had suffered greatly in his life, worked diligently at whatever he did, and so felt himself deserving of all available comforts.

Gradually, The Major took fewer trips. Only one this year, when he returned with presents of a book and telescope. Now he began to drink more heavily, though not by local standards. Sensing his friend's concern, The Major revealed a little of his life: having dead parents and being alienated from a younger half–sister in America. Even his lack of real romantic interest in an older schoolteacher who, the priest knew, yearned for marriage.

But these facts didn't explain his despair. Or, the priest thought, perhaps his ignorance reflected another of his limitations.

He was also puzzled by The Major's odd library: technical journals in the natural sciences and military affairs, weapon catalogs, maritime guides, and customs regulations. In response to the priest's question, The Major made a pun on having "catholic tastes" and returned their conversation to village politics. So the cleric concluded that it, like matters alluded to during confession, were best revealed when ready.

Since returning from New York, The Major tried to forget CATACLYSM by immersing himself in his new Dell laptop. He considered the difference in his life had he been born in Texas and had Michael Dell's talents, for both were in their thirties.

Once, walking beside his horse loving young friend, he noticed that her hair was the color of Letitia's/LeeAnn's and longed to contact his sister but didn't know what to say.

E-mails from his scholars pulled him back to the present. That Gerald's was the first and longest didn't surprise The Major for despite Gerald's reputation being the greatest among his group of scholars he was also the biggest worrier.

"You're probably concerned how things are going," he wrote, which The Major considered an example of the mind's tendency to project painful thoughts onto others, "so here's my first update....

"Things are BETTER than well but I'll let you be the judge. I had planned to begin experimenting in several weeks but an opportunity presented itself...

"A nineteen year old came for a job as receptionist, gossiped of her twenty six month old, and was likely surprised by how rapidly she was hired after my STRONG recommendation." The Major wondered if the sadistic element in Gerald's personality also made him capitalize words.

"While she delivered my mail I offered her candy from a box ten feet away which, when opened, would deliver a weaker version of our virus. She took three pieces. Two weeks later I learned that she and her son were ill, and visited them.

"He had developed a fever and rash, an antibiotic was prescribed and he quickly recovered. She got a headache and milder fever. The doctor thought she had her son's infection and gave her the same antibiotic. At first she was better but she then relapsed with a high fever, chills, nausea/cramps, diarrhea, and a general feeling of weakness. 'I could barely make it to the phone,' she said. Now the doctor had her blood tested.

"Next day she was in and out of delirium and pale with sunken eyes. She was cramped over with an even higher fever and a white cell count nine times above normal, indicating the presence of severe infection. They did exploratory abdominal surgery but the results were inconclusive. Her systolic pressure was seventy two and went up and down like her confusion. They considered toxic shock syndrome (TSST-1) but she lacked a basic symptom: the rash followed by peeling of the skin on her feet and hands.

"They hoped it wasn't TSST-1 for once it is in the bloodstream the only treatment is to support the body's defenses until the system gets rid of it. So they did the usual: intravenous fluids, steroids, heparin, digitalis, oxygen. She recovered, and her case is closed. The virus I used *was* weakened—an odd death would have been investigated. I paid for her child care, lost wages, and coming home present. I said that I would charge all to a company I consult for. Which bill you can expect (g)!"

The Major didn't grin, not having expected a human test to be conducted although, considering Gerald's background as a CIA consultant, this didn't surprise him. The CIA's naturalistic experiments were widespread until congressional hearings and lawsuits in the nineteen seventies.

The reports from Calvin and Heinz were brief and dull. They lacked Gerald's joy in his work. Things were satisfactory despite a surmountable difficulty and needed decision: having to fabricate a fine enough dispersion nozzle, and whether to use two or three disseminations of the virus.

Then came a note from his unknown employer, approving Thanksgiving weekend as the operational date.

Operation CATACLYSM was under way.

BOOK THREE

OPERATION CATACLYSM

Devil's Work

CHAPTER THIRTY

ONE DOWN, TWO to go, LeeAnn thought, as she picked up The Monsters on Sunday night. Despite her long held fantasy about her future married life with Ralph, she had dreaded telling him about her pregnancy. But he turned out to be loving: kissing her belly and, often, asking how she felt. He even made dinner for them which, though just being canned salmon and spaghetti, was something she didn't expect. Having been voted Most Supportive Male Senator by the National Woman's Caucus had never increased his willingness to do household chores in the past.

Valerie's first words indicated her awareness of LeeAnn's changed mood.

"It went well?"

"Great!" said LeeAnn, noting that David wasn't around and The Monsters were busy feeding the cat.

"What did you say?"

"Just that I was pregnant. The words popped out. Easy."

"Like your baby will..." Both smiled.

"Now for your parents," said Valerie, wondering if her mother would tell LeeAnn about her affair with Ralph. "Have you thought of how you'd put it?"

"I'll tell Mom first. Just that I'm pregnant. Not who the father is. He is my dad's *best friend*. I promised Ralph that I wouldn't tell anyone now but you already knew and they should."

"Let's relax with math. I did only half the problems *and* watch your sisters while you had fun."

LeeAnn touched her hand. "Not after I told him. He became like an absent minded husband...maybe because of all the work he brought home with him."

Valerie wondered if they would ever have sex again. Maybe Ralph needed LeeAnn's virginal image in order to get erect, this explaining why he sought a young girl rather than a grown-up woman. She tried not to think about it for the rest of the evening. She wished that both were like other teenagers whose biggest worry was finding a date.

She succeeded, but LeeAnn didn't. Which showed that she wasn't dippy like Valerie thought but just different. She and David made a good couple: both enjoyed analyzing each other's behavior. But LeeAnn only did that when something puzzled her, like now.

Ralph *was* different after she told him she was pregnant, and not just by his playing house hubby. His speech became mechanical and he looked depressed. But he perked up on Sunday, saying that she had cared for him and now he would care for her and their baby. Which was odd since the night before he asked when she would have the abortion. But on Sunday he even promised to get her special vitamins. Which she would take with those David gave her. Couldn't get enough vitamins for two, she concluded.

Lying on the sofa, watching Valerie cook while waiting for David, she supposed it would be like this with Ralph. Then she had another puzzling thought: he didn't ask what doctor she would be seeing.

Arriving home, LeeAnn again considered how to break the news. Telling her mother first still seemed best. She would probably be more understanding than her stepfather even if the other pregnant girls said that both of their parents got hysterical. Hopefully she wouldn't be too drunk.

Elizabeth wasn't and LeeAnn didn't have time to prepare, for like it had gone with Ralph, the news exploded. Fostered by one of her sisters who insisted loudly, "You're getting fat. Are you pregnant?" Which caused LeeAnn to answer softly, "Yes," and her mother's glazed look to frost.

The Monsters continued chatting without paying attention to her response, being more concerned with devouring the peanut butter and jelly cracker sandwiches they were making. The silence between the women continued and, just when LeeAnn thought that she would get upstairs safely, her mother demanded, "who?"

"A man."

"Who?"

"A man," LeeAnn repeated. She related her mother's calm to she not being completely pickled, but dreaded her reaction the next day.

LeeAnn slept fitfully, being unable to relax, and felt comfortable only when she was being fully supported by pillows.

She fantasized Ralph rubbing her back and legs. Then she was surprised at how uncomfortable she would feel asking him to do this for it seemed a greater intimacy than having sex and one they had yet to share. Trying to forget the morning, she anticipated her math test and went over geometry principles in her mind, these being her last thoughts before waking to sunshine which she hoped would mirror her parents' reaction. But her stepfather had already left and her mother was sleeping. As usual.

At school—joy! The math teacher was sick and didn't leave her exam for the substitute who instead spent the hour explaining how to solve real-life problems.

A person should decide what their *values, objectives,* and *goals* were. The importance of being organized yet flexible, and of being able to adjust to new situations by exploring alternatives. LeeAnn ignored the pain in her back and related what was said to her life. Feeling stunned as she realized how wrong she had been.

Believing that Ralph or her parents loved her now seemed bizarre. Her mother, a drunk; her stepfather, a workaholic and drunk too. Ralph, a man obsessed with politics and craving the illusion of youth. Then, looking for alternatives, she recognized that she had categorized them in black/white terms: whether they loved her or not. It was likely that they loved her to the degree they could love anyone, which wasn't much.

And how much did she love her self-centered parents and lover? Probably as little. But she did love her sisters and knew, to the degree children were capable, that they loved her. And she felt sure that she could trust Valerie. So she wasn't completely alone and would make more friends in the pregnancy class. LeeAnn smiled ruefully as she thought this.

Then, as the class ended, she realized that she had been selfish in wanting to become just *a mother*. Going to the few Lamaze classes Valerie could drag her to, saying she was tired but now seeing that this really indicated she wasn't grown up.

Which she vowed to change. Her *values* now were thoughtfulness and self-control; her *objective,* to have a healthy baby; and her *goal,* to be a good mother. Enough!

What *could* she rely on her parents for? She wouldn't know until tonight. What could she expect from Ralph? Here too she didn't yet know. He *seemed* concerned but she knew that all politicians did, and became angry thinking that she might mean just a future voter to him. Although one able to cause him *huge* trouble by going public. Which she would never do for she dreaded having to explain such events to her child. Better poverty than that.

But if her parents wouldn't help she would *have to* ask Ralph. Depressed by this thought, she was kept from walking into the principal, Mr. Silverstein, only by his hands gripping her shoulders.

"LeeAnn!" he exclaimed with mock anger. "Lots of kids try to knock me down but not this early in the morning."

"Sorry. I'm thinking."

"It must be important."

"I'm pregnant," she said, and then mentally kicked herself. Right after vowing self-control she blurted it out. And from the look on his face he wouldn't believe that she was joking. He didn't.

Twenty five years earlier his adolescent girlfriend had become pregnant and barely avoided committing suicide. Fortunately, both mothers supported her decision for an abortion and she eventually became a pediatrician.

Raised in a family committed to education, the principal became America's first black Ph. D. in comparative education, a field whose members possess among the highest intelligence of all the learned professions. His doctoral advisor spoke fourteen languages. He knew thirteen fluently, his Dutch being weak.

After postdoctoral study at Cambridge he was offered tenured appointments at seventeen universities, which is unheard of for a new professor. But he refused all of the offers, choosing instead to head Broad Valley High School. Which required state approval since he lacked traditional certification. Despite union objection this was granted, and Mr. Silverstein became the best paid principal in America. For this was Scarsdale where standards must be maintained. His was also the only black adult face in the building, although there *were* six black students.

The fathers of two of these students were foreign ambassadors, one was the governor's counsel, and the fathers of the remaining three were listed among the *Forbes* Four Hundred Richest People.

One was a former Harvard economics student who abandoned his doctoral study after running out of things to say about his dissertation. He then opened his commodities trading business with earnings from street pickup chess games.

The previous year, after an acrimonious PTA meeting about fund raising, he paid for broad band wiring of the school and added a program permitting students to rent a laptop for five dollars a year.

This successful accomplishment brought him to his next project, for which he felt less optimism: a collaborative effort with a local minister to find a wife for the principal, Joshua Silverstein.

Though a historically Jewish name, Silverstein had long before been adopted by the family in memory of a Southern peddler. Oddly, males in his family were always circumcised and he wondered exactly what help his namesake had given his ancestor.

But the shock which parents experienced upon learning that Mr. Silverstein was black (his name brought him frequent mailed offers of honorary positions in Jewish organizations) wasn't what LeeAnn was thinking. She felt badly at getting another person involved in her trouble. Yet also pleased for she had long yearned *for* a parent and not having to be one.

She sensed that this principal would be more understanding than the typical suburban one. The widespread knowledge of his Harlem childhood aroused frequent school rumors of his drug dealing and pimping, though in a far friendlier tone than with a less appreciated educator. A forehead scar, gained from a razor wielding London mugger, abetted these stories.

"What class do you have now?" he asked.

"Honors English."

"Cut it and come to my office. You already talk better then me."

"Too much."

"Never can tell a friend too much. How do you feel."

"Tired."

"We'll take the elevator."

"What will they think seeing me there?"

"That ancient me has knee problems."

A silly comment for someone only forty two. But kids didn't trust adults who couldn't be silly and LeeAnn had always seemed too grown up. As did so many teenagers with drunks for parents who became great at dealing with practical matters but not their personal relationships. Though saddened by her news, he was glad for the opportunity to cut her slack, as he never did for himself.

His office resembled that of no other school official. Before a bookcase holding foreign magazines was a table on which lay boxes of Health Valley cereal bars. Against the wall was a refrigerator holding cheese, crackers, milk, fruit, ice cream, syrups and garnishings. His sundaes impressed even parents.

"How does strawberry ice cream and syrup with chocolate chips sound? Mint is still considered too black by this community."

"Nothing."

But Mr. Silverstein didn't give up, having learned as a child that problems were solved more easily while eating.

"Cereal bars and milk then, good for the baby."

"Whatever," responded LeeAnn, already feeling better at being mothered.

The principal opened two boxes, apple and blueberry, and dropped the bars onto a tray emblazoned with the cryptic phrase "Elvis Failed Too." Students wondered whether this referred to the singer's success or his descent from it. Even he wasn't sure though Jail house *Rock* was his favorite movie. It was tied with *Clueless* though he never revealed this, fearing that even in this liberal community parents might believe that he lusted after blond coeds. Then he smiled at his imagined retort, "Which middle aged man doesn't?"

As they ate, he ignored the persistent phone ring and finally turned it off.

"What month are you?"

"Sixth. Too late."

"For an abortion? Maybe. Do you want one?"

"Never!"

Mr. Silverstein knew that this decision was usually a poor one, for a baby could never provide what these girls lacked psychologically. Their problems were often why they got pregnant in the first place.

"Who's the father?"

"What does it matter? I've never known mine."

None, he thought, as he remembered rumors about LeeAnn's odd background and made a mental note to ask his secretary, who knew everything.

Fearing that he would make another mistake, he now spoke simply. "How can I help?"

Which caused LeeAnn to think. Criticism and advice she had expected but not this offer. So she responded softly, feeling embarrassed and looking down while speaking. "By being the grown-up I come to when I need one."

"Anytime," he said, thinking that if he ever had a daughter he would want one like LeeAnn.

They sat silently for several minutes. Then, indicating his phone, he scribbled a pass. Later, once again, he concluded to himself that the most successful meetings often contained the fewest words.

CHAPTER THIRTY ONE

LEEANN FELT BETTER. She had thought that Valerie provided her with enough emotional support but now knew that she also needed someone older, like Mr. Silverstein. And she realized that being warm and supportive wasn't just a female quality: men could have it too. He did while her parents didn't, and having Mr. Silverstein on her side made tonight's experience with them easier. Although she expected that it would be worse than it was with Ralph.

It was.

Both parents were home when she and her sisters returned from school. Which shocked her for she had never seen her stepfather on a weekday afternoon before. *And they weren't drunk.* She shooed her sisters upstairs with the promise of elaborate sundaes and hoped that the milk would make them sleepy. Then, too worried to remember to warn them against watching cable movies, she slowly walked downstairs.

She thought of stalling by making a sandwich but couldn't eat. So she walked into the library and sat in the wing chair farthest from her parents.

LeeAnn sensed her mother's orchestration, remembering that she had majored in drama at college, and wondered which play her lines would come from.

"You're pregnant?" her mother questioned, apparently intending to lead off from their interaction on the previous day.

"Yes."

"Who's the father?"

"That doesn't matter."

"It's essential to establish paternal responsibility..." her stepfather began, until a glare from his wife stopped him.

"If LeeAnn says it's not important, it's not. She would be the mother."

Now LeeAnn knew what was coming.

"High school is difficult," her mother continued. "It's *my* fault. I should have been more supportive of you and remembered my teenage years when I became pregnant."

The look on her stepfather's face made LeeAnn think that this news surprised him too, but Elizabeth continued her soliloquy.

"He was older and tutoring me in science. My parents were away and it just happened. During our first time. I didn't think I *could* get pregnant because I was on the pill. But I had tried a few and the doctor said they just didn't work for me.

"Having an abortion is difficult. But it's not as bad as having a baby when you're too young. A girl's body isn't ready and these children are often deformed: mongoloid, retarded. I couldn't take it and won't have you suffer like that. I've let you down and won't again. I'm taking you to my gynecologist for the abortion."

LeeAnn wondered how much of her mother's story was true. The affair sounded plausible, but not the baby. And she never would have gone after a *poor working* student.

Suffocated by the torrent of words and feeling too tired to argue, LeeAnn agreed. A fib to put off their explosion for another week, she told herself. Until after a new suggestion by Valerie or David or even Mr. Silverstein.

"I will have an abortion," she said, "*but it'll be mine*. I'll make the arrangements in New York City."

Her stepfather relaxed and counted fifteen, one hundred dollar bills from his wallet "for expenses." Her mother looked uncertain: things had gone easier than she expected.

"Whatever you say. Then we'll go shopping for grown up underwear at Lord & Taylor. You're too old for Banana Republic."

But LeeAnn knew that her mother wanted to check her out naked.

CHAPTER THIRTY TWO

THE MAJOR WORKED, having long realized that his periods of blinding depression disappeared when he became involved in activity. So he planned while receiving updates from his scholars.

A van needed to be purchased, the personnel hired, and a cover story constructed for *CATACLYSM*. The story came quickly enough to him: a National Aeronautics and Space Administration project studying the ozone composition of the air at sea level. Trying to determine whether seasonal change from two to one part per million now occurred more quickly, the microbes being dispersed being used to increase the accuracy of measurement. A plausible yarn coming with a large enough sum to deter uncomfortable questions, and to motivate the men he hired for work on Thanksgiving weekend.

After receiving his scholars' final reports, The Major met with each to pickup equipment, express "the Pentagon's thanks," and assure them that their final payment would be wired quickly. Though exhibiting no suspicion, all appeared pleased that the project was over. Perhaps he had misjudged their morality, The Major thought. Or maybe their return to routine had already tired them.

Then he sent a present to an old friend of his father in Detroit: a valuable tureen. Following his father's advice that you never know when you might need a place to stay.

While awaiting replies from applicants to the want ads he had placed in four suburban New York City newspapers, he visited this friend to purchase equipment he had long secreted in various European cities though never yet in America.

Racal MA4227 portable telephone encryption units which connect to ordinary phone lines but maximize security. A 9 mm Smith and Wesson pistol and silencer, loaded with Quik-Shok ammunition which rapidly expands for maximum lethality. Alsatex Stun and Zig-Zag tear gas grenades, the former containing a pyrotechnic composition creating a flash effect upon detonation, the latter with jerky propulsion making it uncatchable. Two Steyr AUG 5.56mm rifles, described as an arsenal within a suitcase and capable of rapid conversion from submachine pistol to assault gun.

All fitted within the backing of sturdy suitcases as he drove back to New York City.

For the usual storage problem he chose a common solution: renting a long-term locker to hold these, cash, sets of false identification, and the dispersion nozzles and microbe flasks he had gathered from his consultants. Later, lying on the bed in one of his small rooms which the club extravagantly termed a suite, he wondered what to do until the job applications arrived.

Wandering through this soon to be dying city held

no attraction for him and he felt unable to involve himself in a movie. His thoughts turned to the mother he barely knew, then to his father and half–sister. Soon he found himself once again hurrying towards Grand Central Station to catch the train to Scarsdale, where he arrived in late evening.

After renting a car he drove to the Media Play store where she worked. Then, finding that she wasn't there, to her home. There he watched until, just minutes later, she drove off in a Mercedes SUV. He followed cautiously, being more reluctant than she to speed and risk involvement with the police. Both traveled against the flow of traffic and he managed to keep her in sight by noting the car's outline and pattern of taillights. She left the Harlem River Drive at Forty Ninth Street and turned north, finally entering a building's garage on Beekman Place.

Luckily, a spot opened as he arrived so he parked twenty feet from the building's entrance and waited, again feeling unsure what he sought. More information about her, or what he really felt? Possibly he was just keeping busy to forget the imminent slaughter.

Immersed in thought, he almost missed seeing her leave the building on the arm of a much older, expensively dressed man. Looking like one of the diplomats who frequented the area, but a familiar face. Senator Ralph Beekman: advocate of women's rights, national health insurance, day care for children, and a space based antiballistic missile system whether or not the world liked it.

The Major's dejection was replaced with incredulity: how was LeeAnn involved with *him*? Surely not as a distant relative for the Beekman family history was widely known. Possibly as courtesy uncle, although the pressure of her breast against his arm, until he disengaged, refuted that.

The Major left his car and followed them, concentrating on their shoulders not heads so he wouldn't be facing them were they to turn. Knowing that people and not faces are registered, and he had spoken with her only briefly in a brightly lit store and not a dark street.

The two strolled up First Avenue, stopping first at a supermarket and then at a drugstore. That she carried the shopping bags didn't surprise him for high ranking officials, feminist or not, were always waited on.

Soon all retraced their steps and The Major returned to his car. At one twenty-five in the morning LeeAnn drove from the garage with, The Major guessed, a more relaxed look on her face. Like any protective brother he followed her until she reached home.

An hour later, walking from the garage which adjoined his club, he still felt upset. Having believed her to be a virginal teenager he now discovered her involvement with the most notorious political figure in America. Shaking his head as he opened the heavy door, he missed seeing the dark clothed older figure passing. One more skilled in surveillance and wondering who The Major was.

CHAPTER THIRTY THREE

TOWER WAS COMMITTED to Beekman's political future and not only because of his promise to Beekman's father. Both feared the divisive ideologies threatening America which Beekman would oppose as president. So, feeling certain that publicity of his affairs would demolish the prospect of this occurring, Tower worried about the unknown figure.

"How did you pick him up?"

"Just luck. I was parked across the street when his car pulled in."

"Did he notice you?"

"Please..."

Tower gestured apologetically. "Did you get his picture?"

Dalling removed four, eight by tens from an envelope and Tower remarked on their startling clarity.

"Molulux night vision equipment. Used with *my* single lens reflex camera to save you money."

"How much was the Mod-el-ex?"

Dalling didn't bother correcting him, his thirty percent commission being compensation enough. "Seventy five hundred."

Tower winced though both knew that the photos might be priceless.

"And thirteen thousand for a Riwosa. A Swiss eavesdropping detector. Beekman is being bugged by someone else, using first rate equipment which I left in."

"Later. What do you know about the man?"

"He flew in from Dublin two days ago. Paid for the ticket with a credit card from a bank's private section. No information can be gotten from them: it has one officer accessibility."

"Let's eat," Tower concluded, not wanting Dalling to sense how disturbed he was.

There had been nothing unusual in Beekman's recent behavior. The same playboy charisma overlaying ambition, like with so many senators. Though now he seemed to feel surer of success. But didn't every politician nearing their presidential run?

Tower's anxiety persisted as he sat with Beekman on the following Tuesday, forcing himself to behave surprised upon hearing the familiar information.

"LeeAnn is pregnant," Beekman said.

"Is she having an abortion?"

"No."

"Your decision?"

"No." Now Beekman hesitated, feeling unsure of his lifelong supporter for the first time.

Tower sipped his too strong tea.

"I've thought of marrying her," Beekman said, causing Tower's cup to waver as he wondered if Beekman needed a psychologist more than a manager.

"Just a thought. It wouldn't work," he added a moment later.

Tower calmed. Nothing was changed. "What do you intend to do?"

Beekman paused. "Your advice?"

"I never was a parent. How do you expect hers to react?"

There was a long silence. Beekman was very bright but too self-assured. He was tuned to enlisting others into but not changing his plans, and Tower wondered what he was being recruited for.

"Do you remember Paul Guihard?" Beekman began.

Tower looked past him a moment, then responded "no." Convinced by the care with which the matter was being raised that it was serious indeed.

"I was listening to recordings an hour ago. Calls between Kennedy and Barnett. Remember who Meredith was?"

"The Black veteran enrolled in the University of Mississippi by court order?"

"*After* a pitched battle between marshals and rednecks brought in twenty thousand troops. Guihard was a French–English reporter who was shot in the back. The first of two deaths which so enraged Kennedy that he committed himself to the civil rights struggle.

"Some would say that Guihard had a wasted life. If *you* don't remember him then likely no one except his family does. But his murder changed America. It might even be considered worthwhile since it benefited so many. Like the war that beat Hitler. Wouldn't you say those soldiers died a good death?"

Tower was still puzzled. He was unable to see how LeeAnn's condition related to cherished warriors unless...

"You asked how her parents would react. The stepfather, a well-connected lawyer, would want it kept quiet. But her mother is narcissistic, hysterical. She would try to destroy me no matter what the effect on her family. She'd be on TV within a week. What then?"

Tower was blunt. "Senate censure, certainly. New York prosecution if LeeAnn buckled under pressure."

"She wouldn't," Beekman said, but Tower wasn't so sure. Once LeeAnn found out the truth, both mother and daughter might collaborate on a book of their memoirs. But Tower knew that saying this wouldn't help.

"So you can see there's no alternative," Beekman concluded.

Now Tower marveled at his ruthlessness. So like his father. But how did he hope to get away with murder?

CHAPTER THIRTY FOUR

LeeAnn knew that she looked heavier and so did others. Her mother didn't press her about going for their underwear buying/body inspection trip after her abortion. That evening's absence turned into LeeAnn's attendance at another Lamaze class with Valerie. Who offered to be with her when she told her mother but LeeAnn felt that she had to do it on her own.

So on a rainy Friday she skipped school after lunch and waited for her mother to wake up. Though not hungry, LeeAnn thought of the baby and forced herself to drink milk. She knew, being underage, that she couldn't be thrown out of the house. But also that her stepfather/lawyer could create major nastiness. Like having her be hospitalized for a forced abortion which she had seen enough TV movies to believe was possible.

The sun finally rising over the kitchen's rustic cabinets lifted her spirits. Suddenly her mother entered the room, paddled towards the Braun coffee-maker, and nearly tripped over LeeAnn's long outstretched legs before seeing her. LeeAnn spoke before she lost her nerve.

"I'm having my baby."

Elizabeth didn't immediately understand, having a headache and trying to decide between taking aspirin and drinking coffee. When LeeAnn's words did sink in she became enraged. Not only about she, shortly, would be forced into becoming a grandmother before she could comfortably acknowledge being one. But because LeeAnn had deliberately deceived and defied her. *Which she would learn couldn't be done.*

What flexibility Elizabeth possessed disappeared and LeeAnn shivered as her mother's words penetrated.

"Yes, you'll have a baby. But not this one! I wasn't sure how sensible you would be so I scheduled an appointment with Dr. Gravesell: a psychiatrist who *never* stopped using electric shock. He's been using it to mellow delinquent teenagers in his hospital for a half century. And there's a gynecologist who performs abortions on call."

Elizabeth immediately left the kitchen, feeling that her words would thereby have greater impact. They did.

LeeAnn's nightmare was coming true: her parents destroying both her child and her life. David had witnessed electric shock treatments and said that some patients who endured it became so psychologically damaged that thereafter they could only live with their parents until they died.

LeeAnn's upset caused her to stand up quickly, her uterus to contract and the baby to kick. *My baby not theirs.* Feeling certain that she could no longer remain at home, LeeAnn grabbed her knapsack and walked quickly from the house, dreading having to leave her sisters alone with their parents. After driving quickly to school she took them home, said that she would be going away for awhile and hugged each tightly. Then she left despite their cries, and wondered if she would ever see them again.

She drove slowly after turning the corner, being unsure of where to go, still having the fifteen hundred dollars which her stepfather had given her.

She thought of losing herself in Canada's vastness and felt briefly exhilarated until realizing that, being sixteen, she would be stopped at the border. So she drove to Ralph's apartment, and again considered his initial negative reaction upon learning of their child. Wouldn't her parents' action solve his problem? Not if she revealed who the father was. Which she would do if she were pressured, her resolve strengthening as she entered the apartment.

But Ralph wasn't there. They always met by appointment, as with most things in his life: he might come this weekend or not. Suddenly she felt desperate to talk to someone. Valerie and David were out for the night, "getting to know each other." There was no one except...

Without further thought she dialed Mr. Silverstein, remembering that he rarely left school before six. He picked up on the first ring, expecting trouble from a call at that hour.

"It's LeeAnn. I ran away."

To give himself time to think, Mr. Silverstein asked what he was professionally obligated to ask but doubted that LeeAnn would answer honestly. "Where are you?"

"Safe. I'm waiting for my boyfriend."

"What happened?"

"My parents threatened me with hospitalization and a forced abortion, even electric shock treatment."

"I see." He did, but wondered what he could do. He *should* inform her parents but wouldn't, and fantasized the job he might get after being prosecuted and fired for not doing so.

More silence. Then, again feeling depressed, LeeAnn said, "I just wanted to talk."

"I'm glad you called. I was going to introduce you to the girls in the pregnancy class."

"Not now."

"How long will you be away."

"Until after I give birth."

"Of course. Can you manage?"

"I'll stay here. I still have the money they gave me for an abortion."

He feared that asking for her phone number would cause her to hang up but wanted to give her something to hang onto.

"Take my home number. I always pick up if I'm there. But *don't* get into trouble," he added, after she returned to her phone with a pen. "They once found my number in the Palm Pilot of a student's drug dealer and it took a long time convincing the police that we blacks weren't doing business together!"

LeeAnn laughed, and wrote it down as the door opened.

"I have to go," she said, hanging up the phone.

Ralph looked surprised, as if he were caught thinking something improper. But he quickly smiled and asked, "a friend?"

"Just," she responded, wondering if he was really glad to see her.

"Surprise." Then, since she didn't respond, he changed the subject. "Have you eaten?"

"I wasn't hungry today."

"Mothers-to-be should eat, hungry or not," he chided, and LeeAnn thought of her mother's phony affect. Unable to stop herself, she responded in a bitchy tone, "I wasn't aware that you had been one!"

Ralph looked taken aback and she felt she better apologize. It wasn't good to argue with someone you're dependent on.

"I'm sorry, I'm just worried. Too pregnant too young, like they say. I left home for good." Then she told him of her mother's threats.

To give himself time to think he asked, "What about your sisters?"

"They'll have to get along with them for awhile. Even at five they're smart enough to phone the Hot Line if they have to. Then they'd probably call for a taxi to the State Police."

Her choice of words made him uneasy. To calm her, he rubbed her neck and back. Then, "Will you be all right alone? I have to be in Washington on Monday for a vote." LeeAnn nodded and clung to him as he thought how easily matters could be explained. A distraught adolescent flees her home and seeks the aid of a trusted family friend. Who allows her to stay in his business apartment, planning to mediate the conflict. Then, tragically...

Now feeling relaxed, Ralph enjoyed being with LeeAnn during their last meeting. Cooking for her and asking about her bodily changes. Dr. Gravesell *would* have been an option were Ralph surer of LeeAnn's silence. But he feared what she might reveal during therapy or after the abortion. He smiled as he thought of then losing the *teenage* vote.

In bed, LeeAnn sleepily promised to take the pills he had obtained for her. Which were used by his secretary during two of her *easiest* pregnancies. A fantasized employee but real vitamins. Though soaked in toluene, the active ingredient in a common household product: glue. Causing common pregnancy symptoms: anemia, headache, weakness, dizziness, vomiting. Then blurred vision, tremors, difficulty breathing. Finally, unconsciousness and death. Particularly deadly for infants.

How sad that LeeAnn sought to relax by sniffing glue rather than with the medication which Dr. Gravesell would have welcomed providing her.

He imagined her memorial service. His speech *demanding* adequate counseling funds to avoid such future tragedies. The words ran through his mind. Pauses during which he would be overcome with emotion. Finally, a brief sob.

CHAPTER THIRTY FIVE

LEEANN FELT BETTER after Ralph left. He had been more understanding than ever. Insisting that she remain in bed and bringing her meals there. Reminding her to take his vitamins. Even being reluctant to have sex, as if treasuring her pregnancy. So LeeAnn concluded, for they usually did little but that and eating.

She relaxed as he suggested. Then she got bored and wondered who to call. She couldn't talk to her sisters and also avoid her parents, and hesitated to bother Mr. Silverstein again. So there was only Valerie, who answered on the *sixth* ring.

"Busy?" LeeAnn asked playfully.

"All weekend. How 'bout you?"

"Big doings. OK if I come over?"

"Where else. Where are you?"

"At Ralph's. Over soonest."

Leaving the shower, LeeAnn planned to wear her red cashmere poncho from Lord & Taylor until remembering that she had only the clothes she brought.

Just steps from the bathroom the feelings began, and she barely made it back to bed. Her head felt light and her vision first blurred and then darkened but returned quickly. She remembered David's advice and forced herself to breathe deeply and regularly. Soon the sensation passed and she felt normal again but was thrown by this experience. Her child better be grateful though judging by her sisters' typical behavior she doubted it.

In the garage she again felt dizzy and decided against driving. She asked the doorman to call a taxi and vowing to herself that she would have just *one* baby.

David's apartment was the entire fourth floor of an industrial building which had been converted into lofts for artists. It was located in the up-and-coming NoHo area, which was north of the formerly elegant SoHo. The locked steel gate and intercom belied the million dollar condominiums within.

David's relaxed look was explained by Valerie scooting down the hall in panties and appearing shortly in a phony silk robe. LeeAnn could now tell the difference.

She plopped into the nearest chair, feeling afraid to take another step. A frightening thought considering her usual excellent health.

"You look tired," David said and, surprisingly, sat on the nearby sofa. Regarding her as being Valerie's friend, he usually studied when she visited, despite he now being a frequent weekend father for her sisters.

"I'm just feeling dizzy."

"Are you eating enough?"

"As much as I want to."

David's eyes narrowed but he ignored her challenge. After all, she *was* still an adolescent.

"Are you taking the vitamins I said?"

"Sure, and even something my boyfriend gave me."

"What."

"It was good for his..."

Just then LeeAnn felt a tightness in her chest and fell back. David leaped beside her even as Valerie screamed his name. He took LeeAnn's pulse. It was higher than normal but not greatly so. She quickly opened her eyes, feeling embarrassed.

"Sorry. I'm ruining your evening."

"It was getting dull anyway," Valerie answered, looking worried and holding her hand while David got his medical bag. Then she left to get the orange juice which David asked her to squeeze for LeeAnn so they could speak alone.

"Your blood pressure is a little high. I'll take it again later. Are you worried about anything?"

"Everything!" LeeAnn burst out, and started crying. When Valerie returned she gave David a stare which was meant to communicate "insensitive clod!" Then he sat beside her and said softly, "tell us."

So LeeAnn described her mother's threats, flight to Ralph's apartment, and his oddly changed feelings toward her and the baby.

"Do you plan to marry him?" David asked judiciously. Valerie burst out, "He's an old fart of a senator and is married too."

LeeAnn didn't get angry like she would have just days before. They already knew everything else. So she merely added, "he's not *that* old."

David changed the subject.

"What insurance do you have? If you need an ER."

"The card's in my wallet. In my knapsack." She felt too tired to move.

While rummaging, David came across the vitamins. "Standard stuff," he remarked, reading the label.

"Ralph (no need to conceal his name now, LeeAnn thought) said they helped his secretary to have easy deliveries."

"I can't imagine how," David said, and opened the bottle. He dropped several into his palm and felt them. Though having the familiar red color of vitamins they were sticky with a strange odor. Not the typical sour milk smell.

Maybe outdated, he thought. "Stop taking these. Take only what I gave you and page me if you get dizzy again." Adding with a smile, "you're the only rich patient I have." Then, sensing that the women wanted to be alone, he left with the vitamins.

A thought nagged him as he took the self-service elevator three flights up to the apartment where a painter/single mother lived. Successfully divorced and now seeking her fourth husband, she had once ventilated her problems to David after learning that he intended to become a psychiatrist. Realizing that he was out of his depth with her and hoping to seem wise, he kept silent.

Two years earlier her now fourteen year old daughter scored in the top one percent on a nationwide math exam and was invited to attend summer classes for gifted youth at Johns Hopkins University. After returning home, strange odors began wafting from her apartment, she explaining these as deriving from her chemistry study and intention to become a research physician.

"What are these?" David asked, interrupting her reading of a biochemistry text while she sprawled over three beanbags: for her and the large German Shepherd beside.

"It's obvious," she said, reading the bottle label, "They're vitamins."

"How do you know?"

Sensing his seriousness, she roused herself with conspicuous effort and moved to the farther side of the large room. There, on discarded doors attached to saw horses, were chemicals potent enough to terrify fire chiefs. David watched, feeling teased by the memory just beyond his grasp.

"Quick and dirty?" she asked.

"Quick and sure."

"You need better equipment than I have to be sure but you'd already know if you weren't so uptight."

"*Helen...*"

The girl placed one tablet on a metal plate and touched a match to it. It blazed into ash.

"*Probably* vitamins...but they've been soaked in toluene. It's poisonous and flammable. The benzene smell gives it away. It's widely used as a solvent, and has an odor which is easily recognized by glue sniffers. *Wash!*"

Both scrubbed their hands as David wondered how to respond to her unspoken question.

"I'm doing a favor for a friend," he said.

She rolled her eyes. "*Whatever.*"

"It's not like that. It's too grown up even for me. But when you're a famous doctor you can tell your kids that you saved someone's life when you were fourteen."

"I'll never have kids."

"OK, you'll tell mine. I was helping with your homework if anyone asks."

"Look, I survived three fathers: a lawyer who molested me, a mobster wanting to adopt me, and an advertising genius who lied daily. And I live with my mother. D'ya really think that there's anything I can't handle?"

"Probably not," said David, smiling despite the gravity of the subject. "Lemme see what happens. Memorize my pager number and call whenever. You'll be...Trixie."

She winced at the playful connotation but repeated both name and number and he trusted her photographic memory to retain them. Then he left her: lying on the beanbags, the dog's head in her lap, looking like any typical teenager.

David hadn't yet decided how to get LeeAnn to the emergency room by the time he reached his floor. She and Valerie were making dinner and he wondered what they discussed.

"Men leave," Valerie proclaimed.

"When work arrives," LeeAnn added.

Wanting to puncture the jovial mood but not throw her into panic, David said soberly, "I want to talk to you as your doctor." Then he led her to the sofa and ignored Valerie's quizzical look.

"It's important that you go to the Emergency Room."

"I feel fine."

"The dizziness should be checked."

"You said it's normal during pregnancy."

I'm not doing well, David thought. Then he concluded that she needed to know the facts in order to decide what to do.

"How many vitamins did you take?"

"Just one. The label said one, three times a day."

"They're no good." Again David hesitated, knowing that once he explained there was no turning back.

"Too old?"

"They're...soaked in toluene...a poison...you're being murdered."

The women's calm surprised him and he wondered if something genetic enabled them to cope with crises better than men.

"Tell me," LeeAnn said.

"The chemical's effects mimic pregnancy symptoms: dizziness, weakness, nausea; blurred vision and rapid respiration. Finally, paralysis and death. For you and your child."

"That explains Ralph's change of attitude and his not wanting to have sex," Valerie said angrily. "You wouldn't be safe in a hospital. They'd call your parents and no one would believe you. You're staying here until we figure out what to do."

An English proverb ran through David's mind, "In for a penny, in for a pound." But he knew that Valerie was right. *And no one was going to kill his patient!*

"Drink lots of water," he said firmly to LeeAnn. "At least twenty ounces. Rinse your mouth thoroughly and scrub your hands. That's probably what they'd say in the Emergency Room with just your minor exposure. The baby's probably OK, but you have to rest and do what your doctor says when he checks you. We'll worry about your delivery later."

Both girls visibly relaxed and LeeAnn cracked, "Just like at an HMO."

Now grasping the responsibility he had taken on, David shook his head, "Girl, this ain't nothing like an HMO!"

CHAPTER THIRTY SIX

Rᴀʟᴘʜ ꜰᴇʟᴛ ᴛʜᴀᴛ things were slipping from his control. He had expected to hear news of the finding of LeeAnn's body by now, considering her prominent parents and it being in his apartment. But—nothing. The doorman remembered her leaving in a cab and not returning. So she *didn't* take the vitamins he had elaborately soaked, making another plan necessary.

He was sure that her parents didn't know where she was. He called them and Elizabeth wasn't that good an actress. Damn teenagers for their unpredictably!

She would turn up eventually, with their baby. He couldn't ask the police or FBI to look for her except...if....

He yelled to Tower in the adjoining room.

"When is the next meeting of the Intelligence Committee?"

"Wednesday at ten. Do you want the agenda?"

"I should be prepared."

Tower wondered what caused this unusual sarcasm towards an assistant who was too essential to dismiss.

The conference was ideal, thought Beekman. First, background information from an Assistant Secretary of State on terrorism, followed by a CIA briefing on new technology. There was always an FBI representative present.

Now again feeling confident, Ralph invited Tower to lunch, to amend for his tone. He related it to his stomach distress but Tower wondered.

CHAPTER THIRTY SEVEN

THE MAJOR HAD been instructed by his employer to prepare the van and place it in a rented space, then to FedEx the keys, plans, and all data, including photographs of the drivers he had hired, to an address in Georgetown, Cayman Islands. Their employment proved easy for all of the job applicants had readily accepting his generous fee and cover story. He checked their references to insure reliability, paid half the wages of those he had hired in advance, then practiced them over the lower Manhattan route twice. All were retired from government careers and they looked the image of civil service employees even without the false identification and uniforms he provided them.

All was prepared six weeks before Thanksgiving. Feeling bored, The Major returned to Ireland, to await the catastrophic news which would begin his formal retirement.

Dining at the pub, The Major listened to his elderly friend's advice, using parable as was his style.

"A sultan questioned his wise man. 'I enjoyed glorious travel but arrived home saddened. I had loved the choicest women but these feelings passed. I was disappointed in my new palace. Where can I find fulfillment?'

"The wise man was briefly silent. He didn't want the sultan to think that he was getting cheap advice," the priest added with a smile. "Finally the wise man spoke. 'Sire, you live like the archer who aims far from the target and wonders why he misses. The Great Book says that you must seek Heaven in order to gain Earth. Striving only for worldly pleasure gains you nothing. Great leaders like your father sought godly praise and gained joy, then and in the future.'"

Intrigued, The Major asked, "So what did the sultan do?"

"Maybe he built schools or libraries. Those of Muslims were legendary while Europe wallowed in barbarism."

Feigning shock, The Major asked, "Is that what you tell your parishioners?"

"I do have *some* political instincts though not using them often enough. But what of you? What do you seek? *Truly*. Marriage? Children?"

"No."

"To both? What then? You risked your life for mine when most people would have passed by, yet you seem to condemn yourself mercilessly. You must forgive yourself even without understanding for heaven works in crafty ways."

The Major felt as moved as when his only friend at Devonmere was murdered. So he revealed himself as he had never expected to again.

"I accidentally killed my father protecting a worthless woman. Since then I've been without family or country."

The priest had heard worse in this troubled land where confession was not yet out of style. "Who so makes intercession for the weak, well pleasing is this to Samas...Nothing can change the claims of kinship."

"From the Bible?"

"Babylonian, Anglo-Saxon proverbs."

"You continually surprise me," The Major said softly.

Just then a man demanded that the TV sound be turned up and the resultant blare interrupted conversations. "Americans..." one patron snorted, as all turned to the screen.

"The Director of the United States Federal Bureau of Investigation asks that all be wary of suspicious packages and behavior during the holidays. Fanatic disciples of the long gone Weathermen movement plan attacks on American cities. Many members from wealthy families carried out terrorist and criminal activities throughout the nineteen seventies and eighties.

"A missing pregnant teenager from Scarsdale, New York is being sought. Her name, description, and photograph follow. She should be regarded as armed and highly dangerous and is believed hiding in New York City."

The Major ignored the broadcast, considering it to be a routine holiday warning until hearing the name of the town. Then he looked up to see Letitia's photo. Her home and room were also shown, the camera focusing on a large teddy bear wearing a faded red vest with prominent lettering: DEVONMERE. His anger had chosen this rather than a fanciful name when he made it and he wondered that she kept it.

The announcer continued.

"Following release of this warning, Senator Ralph Beekman, member of the Senate Select Committee on Intelligence and likely presidential candidate, issued the following statement:

'A youth from a prominent family follows the fruitless anarchic path, seeking to destroy all that Americans hold dear. We pray the destruction she and her comrades plan is prevented during these joyful days.

'You can be certain, as you prepare for your festive gatherings, that the authorities are working tirelessly so only those who plan vile deeds will be the ones suffering their consequences. A greater tragedy considering the unborn child who may suffer the consequences of their revolutionary parent's behavior.'"

The screen returned to soccer, the volume was lowered, and the two men resumed eating. Rage swept The Major as he turned to his friend.

"I'll be leaving tomorrow and will drop off a letter before. If you don't hear from me in sixty days, I'll be dead. Go then to the lawyer on Queen Anne's Street. All I have is yours. Use it to make a better world."

On his face the priest saw the look of soldiers prepared for battle. And on other faces, for murder. Knowing that nothing he said could change The Major's decision, he offered comfort.

"Do you remember what you said the night that we met?"

"The Lord protects the guardians of His sheep."

"Yes. I know He does and sense that you have paths beyond this. Can you share where you're going?"

Though unsure why, The Major felt glad that he had asked and said firmly, "To America. To bring my sister home."

CHAPTER THIRTY EIGHT

Mr. Silverstein drew the shades on his office windows, dimmed the lights, leaned back in his chair and closed his eyes. He already felt unenthusiastic about the day since he had been woken at 3:30 A.M. by a crying mother whose son got "only a 'B'" in English and now feared for his early acceptance at Yale. They would meet shortly. At half past ten the union president would learn of the School Board's demand that teachers pay fifteen percent of their health insurance cost in the next contract. Parent anxieties and union negotiation drove him crazy.

He moved towards the snack filled refrigerator, remembered that he was eighteen pounds overweight, so went to the door instead and asked Miss Steelbrill, his secretary, for coffee. Immediately after his hiring she informed him that she served coffee, mornings and afternoons. Though considering this demeaning, he tended to defer to the idiosyncrasies of older people. Also, she made good coffee and he liked being waited on.

His door then being ajar caused him to overhear the most surprising conversation of his career: two FBI agents trying to pump his secretary.

They were contrasts in appearance: tall and short, thin and stocky, hairy and balding. Miss Steelbrill was busy making coffee, had held her job for forty one years and was not to be hurried. After mothering generations of youth who became leaders of numerous industries, she was unassailable, as one principal who wanted her fired discovered. "Her old boys' network is better than Skull & Bones," he snorted, on his last day on the job.

Finally, with the percolator plugged in and cookie tray set, she returned their greeting.

"Visitor's passes," she demanded.

The shorter man gave an ingratiating smile and flashed his credentials. "We're FBI agents and would be grateful for a few minutes of your time. Some of our best information is gotten from secretaries and doormen."

They received the broad smile she reserved for disliked callers and she became determined to make their efforts unrewarding.

"LeeAnn Braxwells is in trouble," the tall man said.

"I didn't know."

"It's been on TV."

"I never bought one."

The agent smiled, this being his default reaction for the people he interviewed who were difficult.

"She's not well."

"She was fine when I last saw her."

"When was that?"

"Two weeks ago."

"Where?"

"Here."

"Why was she here?"

"To speak with Mr. Silverstein. Every student does...sometime."

"Did she ever speak with him before, Mrs. Steelbrill?"

"Not that I recall," she said, becoming angry at his assumption that she was married. Although she could have been—twice!

"We have to find her. She's in danger...from AIDS."

Miss Steelbrill feigned shock and wondered why it only took the presence of a woman to make a man act dumb. "Such a sweet girl."

"They're the most vulnerable ones. She loves New York City. She was walking by the bus terminal..." He nodded knowingly and now began speaking with increasing passion. "Became involved with a black druggie there who preys on blonds. Now she's pregnant and needs help to save her and the baby. We'd never fault her for what she later did. We just want to get her to a doctor...to save her and the baby."

Mr. Silverstein suddenly lost his foul mood, becoming amazed at the agent who believed that he was manipulating Miss Steelbrill. Then he wondered what LeeAnn's trouble really was. Surely not the silly charges although he didn't expect that these agents knew. No one would trust such incompetents with vital information.

Now Miss Steelbrill simpered. "*Mr. Silverstein* will be happy to help you. He's gets *greatly* involved with students like LeeAnn."

The agents smiled as one knocked before both entered the principal's office.

CHAPTER THIRTY NINE

DAVID WAS WORRIED for harboring an accused felon surely placed his license in jeopardy. Now, sitting and drinking coffee on the small balcony, he feared what might happen next. Then he choked as he saw police streaming towards his building and wondered where LeeAnn could hide.

During the apartment's renovation from its industrial roots, its art dealer/owner had installed a fireproof storeroom. The entrance to it lay behind a heavy panel decorated with plaster nudes with the latch concealed within one's well detailed vagina. Which product he considered artful but too politically incorrect to market successfully.

The enclosed sixteen by twenty foot chamber was empty when David was instructed in its secret. Once, needing to study and seeking refuge from Valerie's music, he moved a lamp, chair, and floor cushions there and found it to be soundproof. Then he added a small refrigerator stocked with snacks, thinking that if it had a bathroom too he could rent it for living in this space starved city.

LeeAnn was asleep, clutching a stuffed animal, when he shook her awake.

"The police are downstairs and coming. Quick."

Valerie would have argued but LeeAnn *moved*, grabbing her belongings and straightening the bed (which he didn't think to do). Responses so rapid and assured, unlike those of her mother and stepfather, that he wondered what genes she might have inherited from her dead biological father who no one ever spoke of.

"There's a sound-proof storage room behind the living room wall," he said, prodding her towards it. "With a lamp, food, and plastic bags if you have to pee. Read until they're gone, the book on pregnancy."

Then he waited. Sitting on the sofa and not grasping a word in the medical journal he held.

They wore flak jackets painted with "FBI" letters. A sight which was familiar to him from movies, and David felt oddly knowledgeable.

"FBI. May we speak with you?"

"Sure," he said, feigning surprise and disturbance at the sight of their guns. "What's up?"

"We understand that LeeAnn Braxwells is your friend."

"My friends are all doctors," David said curtly.

"You baby-sit her sisters."

"She's my girlfriend's classmate. We did a favor a few times and were well paid for it."

"LeeAnn is involved in things over her head and we'd like to help her. Do you know where she might be?"

The agent added softly, in a conspiratorial tone, "Her father golfs with Senator Beekman."

"No."

"When did you last see her?"

David thought to lie, then remembered that LeeAnn had come by taxi and the existence of taxi records.

"On Sunday. She left after dinner. I have no idea where she went."

"Can we look around? It's just routine so we don't have to bother you again."

"Sure."

This agent and two others strode through the apartment. Wanting to seem unworried, David returned to his reading. He became more anxious when an agent ran his hands over the wall's carved pubis, though not within it. "Interesting," he remarked to a disgusted colleague. David thought to offer them coffee, then that this courtesy would seem unusual to strangers invading one's home.

The search seemed perfunctory: just one of many. The agent left his card, said that he hoped he wouldn't need his services, and David smiled at this familiar joke. Twenty minutes later, with the window blinds closed and LeeAnn back in bed, he worried that he would need a lawyer.

CHAPTER FORTY

Paul Krasky was unmarried when he became a New York City police officer. When he retired as Deputy Chief thirty six years later he was a widower with five grandchildren he doted on and two divorced daughters who married losers. Whether he and his wife had failed as parents or normality skipped a generation he wasn't sure.

Krasky's parents died when he was three. Lacking available relatives he was, although Jewish, placed in an orphanage operated by Catholic Charities and contracted by the City to house children of all faiths. There he was taught to love Latin by a nun. After graduating from New York's City College and joining the police force, he gained respect from his Italian supervisors for his ability to translate modern curses into the language of Roman legionnaires.

Krasky was awed by the power of words. After talking down a crisis with an armed man he realized that, had his gun been leveled, he might have killed him. Thereafter he became reluctant to draw it but always wore a bulletproof vest.

Because of his low-key manner and ability to communicate, Krasky increasingly came to represent the department with other agencies. He was convinced that crime had both individual *and* community roots, an attitude valued by the New Haven politicians who hired him after his retirement.

Krasky flowered as police chief of New Haven where everyone (except his staff and daughters) adored him. Recognizing the importance of symbol, he changed police uniforms to a less authoritarian style, met weekly with local leaders, and moved into a rehabilitated house in a slum area. Then he announced that he would no longer carry a gun at work. But kept his police driver, and a pistol for when walking through his neighborhood: he wasn't stupid. Nor did he like crises so he wondered what to do with the envelope.

It was ordinary manila and contained typed notes which described a biological attack on a large city and successful testing of the germ. The information was detailed, but omitted the dissemination method and date and location of the strike. After being found in an empty study carrel at the Yale Medical School library, it was forwarded from the dean to the president of the university, and finally to him. Who wondered where to pass the buck.

He didn't believe that any Connecticut city was threatened for none were major and the notes implied a city the size of Los Angeles or New York. A stray thought of his past home town resolved that morning's problem: "Fax these with a cover letter to New York City's new Crisis Center," he told his secretary. Then he opened his collar, put up his feet, and awaited their call.

CHAPTER FORTY ONE

THE CITY LOOKED different, The Major thought, as he left the taxi in front of the club he had never expected to return to. There were more police in the streets and, once again since the World Trade Centers/Washington terror attacks, some carried machine pistols. Which was a common sight in Europe but not here. But people seemed not to notice for the weather was lovely: sunny with temperatures in the forties and ideal for walking. So he also strolled, and wondered where to begin his search for his sister.

All he knew about Letitia/LeeAnn was where she lived, worked, and likely attended school, for those in Scarsdale were so renowned that it was probable her parents considered it unnecessary that she attend one elsewhere.

Despite its affluence, Scarsdale was like any small town where people gossiped and well-dressed strangers with suitable accents were welcomed.

So he returned there in a rented Lexus, knowing that pedestrians were viewed with suspicion in the suburbs. Though malls dotted Westchester County, the town had retained a nineteen fifties sensibility by supporting small shops. Even an ice cream parlor close by the library, which had its own basement coffee bar staffed by volunteers.

He decided to try the library at 2:00 P.M. as his first stop: for gossip with mothers and, after school closed, their daughters.

Bringing recent issues of the local newspaper downstairs, he bought coffee and a mocha frosted walnut/chocolate brownie, then sat at an empty table, being aware of how proprietary Americans were about *their* space. His father once advised him never to sit directly beside a passenger on an American train lest they consider him odd. Unlike in England where a person leaves the outside seat of a three seater empty to aid the next passenger.

After scanning the newspaper, The Major looked towards a woman at an adjoining table. "Keep your distance and smile," his father had also instructed, "people then feel safer with strangers."

"How is Scarsdale as a place to live?" he asked.

The woman returned his smile. She was in her late thirties with straight black hair parted in the middle, like the singer Jewel. She was dressed in gray and wore a gray velvet trimmed cardigan, gray stretch slacks, and gray sporty suit-like jacket. Even her boots and trench coat were a darker shade of gray; only her pink lensed wire framed glasses added color.

"No crime, great people. Do you have kids?"

The Major gave himself a child to focus their talk. "A teen. My wife died when she was six. There's just the two of us."

"You'll feel at home. Most who live here are from someplace else except for those who couldn't get away fast enough and then came back for the kids."

"Vanessa's bright but not sure of herself. Then again...(he made an understanding shrug)...who is at thirteen?"

"*I* was."

Both smiled again. He thought of moving to her table but continued following his father's advice. Then he remembered other instruction he was given: act helpless, women enjoy helping others.

"How is the housing market?"

"What do you need?"

"Four bedrooms. Her cousin visits and one would serve for my office. I've a new software business. I sold the first to spend more time at home when she started getting in with the wrong crowd."

"You'll never regret moving to Scarsdale. People here *help* neighbors. My sixteen year old would *love* taking Vanessa around. My husband is a lawyer. He deals with intellectual property rights. Maybe he can help too." Her eyes glowed with the thought of the stock options he might acquire. "Move to my table so we don't have to yell at each other."

The Major obediently placed his coffee, brownie, and newspaper on her table and his topcoat on an adjoining chair. They exchanged cards. His read Cambium Software. A play on words, he explained, the cambium being the layer of tissue responsible for plant growth. Her husband was managing partner of a Madison Avenue law practice with the undoubtedly valid surname of Smith-Carrollsby.

The woman's daughter arrived shortly. She was dressed like her mother, although in black from headband down, and The Major wondered at this odd style. He bought her an ice cream soda and cookies, assuming that this had the effect on teenagers which alcohol did on adults. And more coffee for her mother, who protested only mildly.

"You're helping *me*," he insisted.

"She'll love it here," the teenager gushed when learning of his situation. "So will you. There are lots of single mothers."

Both adults smiled slightly.

"Vanessa belonged to a gang. They just sat around and smoked which she can't do at home but she's easily led. I want her with kids going to college, not blowing them up."

The girl nodded towards the newspaper's bold headline. "Like LeeAnn?"

CHAPTER FORTY TWO

"LUCK FOLLOWS HARD WORK," his father always insisted. So The Major dissembled more after gazing at the photo and headline: SCARSDALE TEEN CALLED WEATHERMAN LEADER."

"Vanessa's mother wouldn't want that."

Mrs. Smith-Carrollsby scowled at her daughter. "*That's* not Scarsdale. Just someone silly getting pregnant. She'll be at Vassar in two years."

"Along with his big hairy cock!" her daughter burst out to The Major's astonishment, he not knowing how teenage girls talked.

"She said it in her letter!" the girl asserted, returning her mother's stare.

Fearing that her daughter was involved, Mrs. Smith-Carrollsby demanded, "When did you get it?"

"*I* didn't! It was handed 'round. No one's seen her since she started going with that psycho Valerie."

"You're getting a bad impression of Scarsdale. Come for dinner. My husband is home and you have lots in common. Kelly'll invite her friends. You'll see how the teenagers *really* are."

Suppressing his eagerness, The Major said shyly, "I'd be inconveniencing you."

"Nonsense. Is sixty thirty all right? Or would you like to come now?" she asked, not wanting her husband to miss out on what might be the financial opportunity of a lifetime.

"Six thirty is fine. I promised to see some houses."

After giving directions, the mother fled with her daughter before she could say more.

Better and better, The Major thought, as he drove to pick up listings from a realtor. Another of his father's dogmas was to lie as little as possible.

The Smith-Carrollsby home was a modernized ten room colonial on four acres. The dining room's wooden floor was stenciled with flowers amongst geometric shapes, its sense of the outdoors being increased by the presence of plantings and wicker backed chairs.

The Major vaguely described his computer products as exceeding current security capabilities without effecting system stability. Then he reacted enthusiastically to his host's story of having sued a publisher who, after asking an author to review a newly published but unknowingly plagiarized book, was told by him, "*I* wrote this twelve years ago."

Over dinner the teenagers expressed joy at the sedate life in Scarsdale, apparently having been sternly instructed by Mrs. Smith-Carrollsby. The Major described Vanessa as he imagined LeeAnn to be, and wondered how to get the girls alone in order to shift the conversation towards her.

Again, he lucked out. After their petulant demand for ice cream, he offered to drive them to the local shop, seeking (he explained) to view the town through adolescent eyes.

Their caustic comments described Valerie's decrepit car and small house and gained for him her address. Then they gossiped about LeeAnn. All considered the reports describing her as being a terrorist to be nonsense. She had no interest in politics and, until recently, was one of the oldest virgins in school. If she changed it must be because of her boyfriend, who nobody knew. All agreed that she would make a good mother since she had raised her sisters. Both of her parents were drunks, and her mother had tried to seduce a minister!

After gaining this information so easily, The Major questioned why LeeAnn was still being sought.

"We'd never tell anything!" one stated emphatically, and the others nodded their heads.

The ice cream they demanded was his by far smallest payment for information, he thought, before falling asleep at a motel. He planned to follow Valerie the next day, using their description of her car.

That afternoon, waiting in the school's parking lot, he worried most about LeeAnn's response. She *should* welcome his aid for she was now involved in something far beyond the ability of any teenager to cope with. But he learned last night that adolescent behavior could be illogical.

What if she blamed him for not having rescued her earlier from her miserable family life? Or, being desperate for warmth, if she *had been* seduced into aiding terrorists. Maybe both.

Valerie entered her car soon after two and drove towards New York City, her destination being an old factory building. After she entered it The Major double-parked briefly, jotted down all the names on the intercom, and then parked where he could view the building's entrance.

Just after seven the lights went out on the fourth floor, she left, and he followed her back to Scarsdale. Being intent not to lose her in the now heavy commuter traffic,

The Major didn't notice the car following his. And he would have felt less pleased with himself had he heard the brief phone message from it: "Our boy is back."

CHAPTER FORTY THREE

MOFTON DISTRUSTED OTHERS' conclusions. And particularly those of the inexperienced idiots he faced. But he listened carefully while they guzzled the Krispy Kreme donuts he brought for his staff each morning.

"Tell me again what the principal said," he softly demanded.

"He admitted that he knew about her pregnancy but not who the baby's father is or where she is now."

"Did he seem nervous? As if he wanted to help?"

"He looked bored," the other added. "His secretary brought him coffee. He didn't offer us any."

"Did you question her?"

"First. I said that LeeAnn got AIDS from a black druggie and we were trying to help her." Mofton momentarily closed his eyes. "It burst out," the agent pleaded.

"Like the archetypal black mugger described by the murdering white husband in Boston. Did you tell this to Silverstein?"

"He's...black."

"That must have been a shock to you. So he overheard, you got nothing, and I must travel to Scarsdale."

Then, feeling the unwarranted guilt he too often experienced after criticizing subordinates, Moften exhibited that tact which had made him the most popular director in decades of Manhattan's FBI office.

"But I need country air anyway. When questioning someone, always view the situation from their point of view. Be folksy, but don't say anything which could embarrass you in court. And *try* to avoid generalizations."

Later, Mofton's thinking turned to that day's emergency meeting at the Crisis Center. He wondered if these would be less frequent after the election. Maybe more, depending on who won: some mayors liked to be seen managing crises on TV.

He drove there quickly, then spent a half hour walking about the neighborhood's shops which, even after nine years, still entranced this native of Smyrna, Georgia. It seemed inappropriate to place the new Crisis Center so close by where the last one was destroyed. But perhaps this was meant to carry symbolic meaning. Or maybe the space was leased cheaply, and government workers also loved the area.

Patel, the Crisis Center's director, opened the meeting by describing their new computer upgrade, as if he were speaking to reporters. Then he plunged into the matter at hand.

"A plan for a C-B attack on some large city was discovered in New Haven and forwarded by their police chief. a former New Yorker. Copies are in your packets. I suggest we read it."

They did.

Deputy Police Commissioner Conklin commented first. He didn't like civilians being involved in what he regarded as police matters.

"How long have you had this?"

"Since yesterday," Patel shrugged, expecting an onslaught of criticism which, however, didn't arrive. Conklin was planning for his retirement and had begun to behave more tactfully with politically well-connected civilians.

Then the stranger spoke. His nameplate read Johnston but Patel tripped over the name and the others wondered what it really was.

"Washington is grateful for the prompt notification by Chief Kransky and has more recent information. The target is Manhattan and the weapon is an altered virus. With potential casualties in the six figure range."

"Suggestions?" asked Patel into the shocked silence.

"Vaccination?" asked Mofton.

"Not for an unknown germ," responded the only female member of the group. Her qualifications included Board Certification in Internal Medicine and membership in the Abraham Lincoln Republican Club, an unusual combination in this Democratic city.

"We'll cancel leaves and have police on every block," Conklin boasted.

"Wearing space suits, and looking for what?" the doctor scoffed.

"It'll kill tourism during our busiest season!" Dilby, the Assistant to the Mayor, added. "We'll lose billions because of a sci-fi story. How many threats do we get a year, Chief?"

"Forty to sixty."

"How many attacks since the World Trade Centers destruction?"

"None."

Mofton looked down at the report as Johnston spoke. Slowly, and with certainty.

"I suggest that we meet every other morning. Then daily, after martial law is declared."

"We can't use soldiers to shoot a bug." the doctor insisted. "They can be spread using gadgets the size of credit cards."

Patel closed his loose leaf and stood. "Wednesday at eleven?" he proposed to his silent colleagues.

CHAPTER FORTY FOUR

LEEANN FELT LIKE she was going crazy and being alone just made it worse. Since the FBI's visit, David insisted that she hide in the storeroom all day until he returned. Reading. Eating. Mostly staring at the whitewashed walls and listening to the ventilation system which, David assured her, had protected art and so was at least adequate for her and her baby.

To try to keep sane, LeeAnn implored the upstairs genius, Trixie/Helen, to stay with her on the frequent days that she was out of school. The current "suspension until placement" followed her loud announcement that a math teacher's confused logic reflected his need for retirement. Only the principal's uncertainty whether she suffered from "conduct disorder" or "hyperactivity" had delayed her placement in the Chronic Dysfunctional Program along with the other misfits.

Within minutes after David's introduction of them, the girls bonded. LeeAnn recognized that it was Trixie's shyness and social naiveté which created her problems. And her brilliance: she was awed by Trixie's knowledge.

After reading to LeeAnn for an hour from an infant care book, Trixie tossed it aside and asked, "How do you flirt?"

A question which still puzzled LeeAnn since she had never been sure who made the first move with Ralph though knowing that it shouldn't have gone further. But, being older than Trixie, she wasn't about to reveal her ignorance and quickly thought of all that she did know. She felt ashamed that it wasn't much.

"Boys are dumb."

"Most people are," Trixie responded, placing her arms behind her head and sprawling, hungry for girl-talk.

"Not just compared to you but with girls, so you have to teach them."

"I thought we were talking about flirting."

"We *are*," LeeAnn said, feeling exasperated like she so often did with her sisters. Then she reorganized her information.

"They don't act straight."

"I only want a straight guy."

"*Trixie!*"

"OK, OK."

"As I was saying. They're not sure how, so you have to help them. A guy at a dance likes you but sits in a corner reading. What should you do?"

"How do I know he likes me?"

"Because sometimes he looks at you but mostly he pouts and when you look at him he turns away."

"A creep."

"No, he's just shy. Like you are sometimes. So first you decide if you might like him, and then..."

"I sit next to him."

"Good. And..?"

"Duhhhh..."

"*You* talk to him. About something deep like politics or art. Remember that he's more scared than you are so it may take awhile for him to open up."

"One more," LeeAnn said, already having tired of being the big sister. "The guy who dances on a table at parties and always jokes."

"Why would I want him?"

"OK," LeeAnn thought quickly. "How about the one who stares and gives you compliments?"

"I stare back."

"Right! But also thank him and say how much his remarks mean to you."

"What if they don't?"

"Tell him anyway."

Sensing this topic was exhausted, Trixie turned on their small TV in time for the "latest breaking news" about LeeAnn and the other anarchists.

"Once again heightened fear over terrorist activity in Manhattan has prompted a startling suggestion. That there be identification checks of school girls, who have already been issued picture IDs. The mayor vowed that *any* disruptive behavior would be treated with as great severity as the police exhibit towards drunken drivers. Raising the unanswered question from this reporter of whether boom boxes would now be seized as quickly as autos."

Trixie switched the TV to a tape she had made from the Romance Channel. Both loved the story about a guy who finally falls for the right girl who stayed his buddy even when he loved the wrong one. They were tearful at its end and LeeAnn felt more alone than ever, wondering if things *would ever* straighten out.

Just when she felt she couldn't feel worse, a shattering pain rippled through her belly, then tapered off only to begin again.

Noting the look on her face, Trixie rushed over.

"Baby's coming," LeeAnn gasped.

CHAPTER FORTY FIVE

THE SENATOR, WHICH was how Ralph Beekman viewed himself despite there being ninety nine others, had believed that LeeAnn would be quickly located, considering the massively increased government resources which were being allocated as public hysteria multiplied. This resulting (he was sure) in at least one death, followed by his moving speech praising the law enforcement community.

But he wondered why it took so long to find a naive sixteen year old with few friends. He feared another WACO disaster after reading the FBI's report of its farcical contact with Mr. Silverstein. Their proposal to introduce youthful agents as students seemed more a failed TV script. And trust *that* principal with a secret now!

Feeling depressed, he asked Tower to come into his office. Beekman's mood was lifted just by the presence of this old man, who reminded him of his father.

"How good are your sources?"

"For what?"

"To find LeeAnn at whatever the cost. She and her baby will be a continual threat."

Tower risked a small smile. "My first campaign task?"

"The last one if you fail."

Tower played with his cup of tea, thinking of Ralph's hunger for the presidency. He remembered his promise to Ralph's father, so he wasn't surprised by his words.

"Your campaign already has an intelligence section to avoid surprises like this. She's hiding in a fourth floor condo on Jay Street in New York. She's staying with the doctor/lover of her girlfriend, and never goes out."

The usual smile lit Ralph's face. One which was so winning that who spoke with him would leave convinced of his talent and commitment to their cause.

Ralph gently squeezed the old man's shoulder. "Once again my only true friend, I owe you."

Tower shook his head. "We both owe your father."

CHAPTER FORTY SIX

THE PRIEST'S QUESTION echoed through his mind as The Major lay on the bed. What did he want? Even as he knew that his frequent response to himself, to save Letitia, was incomplete. He barely knew her and had now returned to a nation seeking his death. Then a memory: she gazing upwards towards him with complete trust. As he had in his father.

"I must change my life," The Major told himself aloud. He felt with this statement a sense of closure, and that the part of his personality which lay stunted since he left Devonmere had now awakened. Then he wondered what to do.

Letitia was probably in the apartment which Valerie visited and he needed to investigate this. But first to destroy the microbes, to give himself more time and prevent the horror it could cause.

He phoned his father's Midwest acquaintance. "Detroit," his father had nicknamed him.

"The weather is becoming difficult."

"What do you need?"

"Something to protect my face. Send it to Suite S6. Along with three heaters. I'm used to the blazing tropical temperatures."

"Will Tuesday be soon enough? I'm passing through and can drop them off."

"Fine. We'll eat where we last met with my father. At five, before it gets crowded."

"I remember."

Though distrusting phone security, The Major doubted that anyone could interpret their conversation: the instruction to bring one Leyland and Birmingham S6 Anti riot Respirator, which was protective against biological hazards, and three thermite bombs.

The technical problems were the easiest to solve, his father always advised, so he had left consideration of the others for last. How to establish and keep Letitia/LeeAnn's trust after eliminating her friends; and how to get her (including possibly a baby) through the garrison the city was becoming. He knew that if he could find her it was only days, maybe just hours, before the authorities did.

All in all, The Major concluded, it would take a miracle. Then he smiled as he remembered his elderly friend's statement that times of misery and miracles tend to bunch together.

Walking a dozen blocks brought him to the parking lot holding the virus disseminating van and his new problem: it was gone.

CHAPTER FORTY SEVEN

RALPH LOVED BEING senator and didn't doubt that being president would be better. Not for the personal service he had always enjoyed, but for the power to impact on America. Then he remembered a story which Tower once told him. President Ford had ordered that the taping equipment which sparked Nixon's downfall be removed. Weeks later it remained, waiting for someone to flick the switch and Ford wondered if anyone did. "Power doesn't translate easily into action," Tower concluded, in this early lesson.

Which was why Ralph had ordered an elaborate buffet for the next Crisis Center meeting, hoping this would make others amenable to his suggestion. And why not? The ensuing glory would be theirs.

He deliberately came a half hour late, believing that it would be best for their persistent conflict to block decision until his information molded their agreement into line with his plan.

Patel's heap of banana peels and bagel remnants reflected his vegetarianism and stress. Beside him, Krasky calmly drank tea: this wasn't New Haven's problem.

Mofton and the doctor, both single and apparently attracted to each other, held their heads inches apart as the Deputy Police Commissioner argued loudly with the mayor's assistant. This was an odd sight for they were usually allies.

The military was represented by National Guard Colonel Braleigh, commander of a Weapons of Mass Destruction Civilian Support Team which was established after the first World Trade Center bombing. Beekman had co-sponsored the bill funding twenty seven of these units, and added Tower's suggestion that they be placed within the National Guard so that the military would not be performing police duties and thus violate federal law. The units were intended to help local governments after a chemical, biological, or nuclear threat.

"We can't destroy this city's economy because of *potential* events," the mayor's assistant insisted.

But the Deputy Police Commissioner knew who would be blamed if anything happened.

Johnston's statement ended the argument. "The president and governor have decided. The National Guard will be federalized and patrolling Manhattan in five days unless they're caught."

I couldn't have choreographed the scene better, Ralph thought, having arrived and offered effusive greetings two minutes earlier.

"Gentlemen, Doctor," he began. "My sources have located the teenage terrorist and her followers. They're staying in a condo from which reports of odd chemical odors were long ignored."

Then he distributed loose leaf binders which were handed to him by his current gofer, a lush nineteen year old.

"These contain blueprints from the architectural renovation of the building. Their weapons include phosphorous grenades and silenced MAC-10's. With booby-traps all over. They vow group suicide if caught. The nation expects you to treat these vipers mercilessly."

The doctor's objection, that LeeAnn was but "a pregnant child," collided with Ralph's statement which caused adoption of his plan. "But one who is willing to murder thousands," he boomed.

CHAPTER FORTY EIGHT

"**WE'LL MAKE AN** obstetrician of her yet," David said, teasing to hide his concern. "How long did the pains last?"

Trixie shrugged. "For fifty six minutes. The longest was thirty seconds. No fluid loss."

"False alarm. They're Braxton Hicks contractions. Real ones last more than forty seconds."

LeeAnn lay in bed feeling, despite their youth, no different than when she lay on her pediatrician's table. Her due date was a week and she felt increasingly vulnerable, now thinking more of her lovemaking with Ralph. Then she reminded herself of the similarities between that and pregnancy: contracting uterus, deep emotion, moaning. She was definitely less inhibited: now she listened calmly to her friends discussing the state of her body!

LeeAnn felt glad to be out of her tomb, which was what she considered the storeroom she hid in. For weeks she had dreamed of lying paralyzed on her cot while a tall man approached with a gun. David interpreted the dream as meaning that she was anxious: from her normal fears about childbirth and those from the rest of her life which would terrify anyone.

LeeAnn sensed that she would have a healthy baby, but then what? To live forever with Valerie and David? Or to attempt to flee, with her picture being everywhere?!

A week before, when she felt *really* depressed, she slipped to Valerie her thought of killing herself. Valerie told David this and David advised LeeAnn that this meant she was feeling poorly about herself. Which was caused by her lifetime of lousy parenting and not the present events, though they were certainly bad enough. LeeAnn felt better after their talk but the thought of suicide had returned, though she knew that she would never harm her baby or the mother it needed.

So, doing battle against her parents and the most powerful government on the planet, LeeAnn did the only thing making sense: she prayed. Not for her life which she considered nearly over. Only, *somehow*, that her child survive and, *someday*, learn how much she had loved him/ her. Which would make everything she endured worthwhile.

She forgave her parents and even Ralph, asking that they and her sisters and friends find good lives. Then she fell into a dreamless asleep, as the Crisis Committee weighed her death.

CHAPTER FORTY NINE

"Prepare for the improbable," advised his father, and The Major had. Having told the salesman that he often needed to locate his unpredictable sister, The Major was described the twenty four satellites which enabled the Global Positioning System to determine a car's location. The dealer installed the Mobile Watch beneath the van, advising against purchase of the TravelEyes model with its shorter (twenty driving hours) battery life. "Who knows where she'll wind up?" True enough.

The Major had preferred the military Centurion model which could locate a car within fifteen feet. But Mobile Watch's hundred foot range was good enough, and readily available on the civilian market. Finding the van meant simply plugging a card adapter into his laptop for a fifty second data transmission. It was parked in Yonkers, by the home of a driver applicant.

The restaurant was vastly changed from years before. Shimmering lime table tops set on stainless steel bases caused the tableware to appear as if it were floating.

The curved wooden ceiling, translucent panels holding the bar's wine display, and video monitors playing customers at the entrance were very twenty first century. Both hoped that the food had remained classical.

They spoke pleasantries while the charcoal gray uniformed waiter took their orders, each taking the measure of the older men they had become.

"You resemble your father," Detroit said.

The Major nodded. "What happened between you?"

Sadness glanced over Detroit's usually impassive face. He began eating his baked potato, then put down the fork.

"He saved my life. I wanted to save his."

The Major waited, sensing a story was unfolding.

"Think of man's glory. Mine was that I had such a friend."

"You're corrupting Yeats," The Major said with a smile.

"I was in *KRAN 19*."

A memory associated with this phrase escaped him. The Major shook his head and Detroit resumed speaking.

"It was a unit of discharged Army lieutenants which was hired by the CIA. They were trained and inserted into Laos and North Vietnam for study and operations. We were losing fighters to surface-to-air missiles and Washington wanted confirmation that they came from Russia. The order was to get next to them and to note their markings for propaganda points. It was a one man mission into the no-man's land of Southern China from which no one returned.

"From reconnaissance photos they picked a plateau overlooking a major intersection, thirty miles north of the Chinese/Vietnamese border. Air America would drop me from a stripped-down DeHavilland Caribou. The mud in the road would slow the trucks and make my opportunity.

"It was as crazy as it sounds. Drop from six hundred feet, climb trucks stuck in mud, radio the markings, and get home. The usual boondoggle planned by politicians. I looked at the photos and couldn't see most of what was claimed in the briefings. If I was hurt landing, before dawn in a light rain, I'd be captured and gone. I carried no identification and wasn't on any roster. Dig a shallow grave and take your suicide pill was the word.

"Even if everything went great, would they *really* rescue me in Chinese airspace? Risk China's intervention in Vietnam and possibly cause World War III? I wouldn't bet on it. And the extraction method was new: a tail hook grabbing onto my bungee system to crank me up.

"They bear-hugged me before I left but no one said much. We'd been pushed beyond sentiment and this mission was different. Before, we worked at least two together. Now I was alone in this insane war where everyone said 'don't be afraid to die or there when it happens.'

"Then came their final order: to photograph the SAM missiles' markings using flash, which would attract soldiers from a mile away. I agreed, but left the camera behind. Why not refuse to do it? Because I depended on them to bring me out. But even the pilots didn't want to go once they learned the mission.

"I did my usual on the flight in. Repeated the plan in my mind, then tuned it out. I thought of my sister barging into my room, my mother baking, my father finishing the basement—his lifelong project. They're all dead now. Sister at seventeen from leukemia.

"The jump went fine, the ground was mud and grass, and the radio contact was OK. I was a half mile east of the plateau and away as soon as I buried the chute. Then I climbed a tree to wait for light. The fog lifted and I saw convoys of trucks but nothing heavy enough to carry SAMs. These trucks came three days later pulling twenty five foot trailers. Suddenly all stopped, with everyone except two drivers and a helper leaving. Probably to help free other trucks stuck in mud up the line.

"I walked to the second truck, which wasn't as dangerous as it sounds. It was early evening and my light skin wouldn't stand out from a distance. I'm also smaller than most Americans, was dressed in their tan uniform and held an AK-47. Along with a silenced .22 pistol under my shirt.

"I climbed into the cab. The driver woke, looked at me groggily and tried to make sense of what he saw. My bullet hit him in the forehead and he slumped over. I left, bowed slightly as if I were saying good bye, then inspected the missiles.

"Which *were* Russian. They had definite Cyrillic markings on their top. I'd just left the truck when I was hit by a rifle butt. I landed on the ground facing two white men babbling in Russian. They'd left the other truck and saw the dead driver. One found my pistol, walked behind his companion, and shot him in the head. Then he said, "we'd best be going." He was English, not Russian. He was your father."

The Major carefully placed his wine glass down as Detroit continued.

"It took us six days to get back. Eating grubs and snake. Traveling nights, sleeping days in trees. He was older and I worried about him. A SEAL unit took us out by the Red River, north of Lao Cai. They wouldn't get my answer until they did.

"Before he left I asked 'why.' He looked back. 'Because you're an American and I'd want you fighting beside my son.'"

"But he sold to the Chinese!" The Major insisted.

"And brought back better information."

The Major absorbed this. "How did you try to save his life?"

"I told him what I thought of your stepmother. He never spoke to me again but our agreement stands: with his son to whatever end!"

The Major felt so greatly moved that despite his dislike of casual physical contact he gripped Detroit's hand.

"You've come for Letitia?

The Major nodded.

"You'll never get her out alone."

The Major considered his offer, then the tremor in his hand.

"From aging, not Parkinson's."

The Major shook his head slowly. "She may not come. I'll let you know. My heaters?"

Detroit indicated the suitcase by his leg. He almost had to slug the solicitous waiter to keep it with him.

"I made something special for you. How much do you know about thermites?"

"Just how to detonate them."

Detroit relaxed: his teaching ability had made him the most popular science instructor in the Grosse Point school district.

"They burn above fifty four hundred degrees. This is caused by a reactive metal reducing oxygen from a metallic oxide. They're safe to store, not being shock or friction sensitive, and they ignite at two thousand degrees. I've made you the best: *hellhounds.*"

The Major nodded appreciatively as Detroit continued.

"A fuel-air explosion beginning with its electrical ignition by timer. The thermite burns and super heats the gas surrounding it which the container keeps from boiling. After reaching the explosive the fuel expands and mixes with the air in a mist. They're four pounds each. For someone you particularly dislike?"

"An empty van."

"But not completely."

The Major nodded and they finished eating in silence. Leaving the restaurant separately, Detroit walked several steps, returned, then grasped The Major's shoulder and whispered into his ear.

"Your father lived for his kids. If there's a God above the heavens are moving to save her."

CHAPTER FIFTY

RALPH HAD OFTEN COMPARED his actions to those of former presidents, and prided himself on remaining calm while the weightiest matters advanced. Though he disliked being alone.

"By one-ten tomorrow morning it'll all be over. 'The objective is the thing' as Truman said."

Tower noted that he omitted the rest of that statement, "not personal aggrandizement." Or, as George Elsey who ran the secret White House map room during World War Two reported, "He didn't care who got credit so long as the job got done."

"They'll use dartcord cutting explosive for getting in. Then machine gun everyone, using flame throwers to kill the bacteria. It'll take a little luck but where can she go in her condition?"

Tower was surprised by the depth of Ralph's anger. He concluded from this that Ralph had loved LeeAnn deeply and was now projecting his rage onto her—*blaming her* for making him effect her murder.

Knowing how slowly groups operate, Tower didn't expect their decision to be made this quickly so he needed to speed up his plan lest the truth become known. After telling Ralph that he needed to have his hearing aid checked in New York City, he called Dalling who was watching LeeAnn's building.

Seeing the traffic light suddenly turn red as he left New York's Pennsylvania Station, Tower was struck by the thought that the problem which LeeAnn's existence created would soon end nearly as quickly.

CHAPTER FIFTY ONE

TERRORISTS DEMOLISH VAN

YONKERS, NOVEMBER 24 Dwellers east of the Industrial Park area were awakened at 2:15 A.M. by a powerful explosion which gutted a van and produced a three foot crater. Nearby cars were set ablaze but there were no injuries.

Mrs. Amelie Etzioni, an eleven year resident of the area, described the scene from her bedroom window as being "like a war movie. Trees and cars were burning. My nine year old walks to school and I'm shaking what could've happened later."

Another resident, who wished to remain anonymous, was walking his dog when he heard a thunderous blast followed by others. "I was a block away. The street lit up like an explosion from hell."

Calls flooding the police emergency line caused fire companies from North Bronx, Mt. Vernon, and Bronxville to be summoned. Thermite residue in the debris supported what officials had long feared: the beginning of a wave of bombings to terrify civilians and mold government action.

Roused from sleep, Governor Valenti forcefully proclaimed that "such activity won't diminish our resolve that these monsters be extirpated. Once again the Empire State will exhibit to all Americans that steel ingrained by our forefathers and revealed during time of crisis. A danger believed contained within New York City threatens the state's northern suburbs. As a precaution, martial law has been extended to all counties south of Orange and Dutchess."

New York's junior Senator Beekman, interviewed at his New York City apartment while monitoring the deepening crisis, described City inhabitants as being calm and predicted that the Weathermen responsible would be quickly apprehended.

"America loves its children but for those engaged in murderous acts we have this warning: your terrible end is near. Cease this behavior and rejoin all citizens to help create a better land."

CHAPTER FIFTY TWO

THE CONTRACTIONS NOW LASTED more than forty seconds. Twenty, fourteen, and finally ten minutes apart. Trixie was scared but did what David said to do if he wasn't around. Encouraging LeeAnn to walk, and supporting her when contractions occurred. Serving her bouillon, David having said that the American custom of prohibiting food during labor arose when women were made unconscious during childbirth. Massaging LeeAnn's neck, shoulders, and calves, and assuring her that she was doing fine and would have a healthy baby.

Trixie wondered how she had developed these capacities with her everything but maternal mother. Though feeling worn out herself, she continuously reminded LeeAnn to take regular breaths and encouraged her to talk about her feelings.

Trixie had read that many childbirth practices were the equivalent of ancient ritual, like unlocking doors during a difficult labor. Still, she wished that she had such a key.

Contractions became sixty to seventy seconds and at two to three minute intervals. Trixie couldn't find a comfortable position for LeeAnn, who became increasingly irritable. Her legs trembled and Trixie massaged them from groin to knee, then applied warm compresses. She had to pee but was afraid to leave and wanted to cry.

So did LeeAnn, who felt that she was experiencing too much. Not formerly being intuitive, she had become so during pregnancy, gaining increasing awareness of subtle bodily sensations as she bonded with her unborn child and matured from woman to mother.

She worried more too, having had another dream in which someone came to murder her. Probably Ralph, she thought, trying to dismiss the memory.

"Busy times," David said jovially as he glided into the storeroom, "but *always* shut the door." Trixie's anxiety turned to anger as she noted that *he* had just left it open.

"How's my mother-to-be?"

"Contractions are seventy seconds apart with increasing frequency. The late first stage of labor," Trixie said.

"You'll be a great doctor."

David was glad that he wasn't alone. He had hoped some way could be found to get LeeAnn into a hospital. His last delivery seemed years before and skimming obstetric texts didn't increase his confidence. But then he became calm by reminding himself that nature would do its job well, as it nearly always did.

"How are *you*?" he asked Trixie, whose face reflected her limit of endurance. It was good that his last two patients had canceled. She shrugged, and he squeezed her shoulder.

"How long since they began?"

"Four hours."

It won't be long now, David thought, as LeeAnn screamed from pain.

He dimmed the light and moved her onto her side, having Trixie hold her top leg up. Speaking softly and slowly while she pushed.

"I want you to breathe deeply and to relax. *Feel* the relaxation flowing through your body *from* your head...into your stomach...*then into your feet.* As it flows, imagine yourself as a beautiful lily...opening...petal...by...petal. A warm sun shines over you, coaxing you to open while birds sing softly in the distance. *Take another deep breath and,* as you breathe deeply, *inhale* this soft sunlight into your womb. Now it surrounds your baby, *encouraging it* to leave. The warmth radiates through you and your tension leaves as your body *opens more and more.* Feeling *more and more* relaxed as your baby moves into the world."

While he spoke, despite her increasing pain, LeeAnn's face smoothed and she raised her leg further. Her breaths became panting and she held them and bore down. Soon the baby's head appeared, then receded slightly, her cervix opening wider with each contraction.

"You're doing fine," David said encouragingly. You can stop pushing. Just pant gently."

Trixie thought that the baby's wrinkled face looked angry. It rotated to the right spontaneously and its shoulders began to appear. Then contractions resumed and the rest of the baby exited: it was a boy.

David suctioned the mucus from his mouth, clamped and cut the umbilical cord, and washed him. Then he rated the Apgar score. Nine out of ten: a healthy child.

After cleaning and covering LeeAnn, he handed him to her. She spoke sounds generated since human beginnings, then placed him close to her breast and he rooted for her nipple. Soon she dozed, but became aroused by a slight noise from the other room, which was ignored by David and Trixie who were engrossed in their medical talk. Moments later, two men dressed in tan maintenance uniforms approached the doorway. Holding what she recognized from movies as being machine pistols. One was the figure from her nightmares.

"Have you come to murder us?" she asked into the shadows, trying to shield her helpless son with her body.

CHAPTER FIFTY THREE

Senator Ralph Beekman lit an unfiltered Camel and felt the same thrill that he had forty years earlier, during his innocent days. This cost far more but the goal was worth it.

Soon: "The President of the United States requests..." "Mr. President..." Invitations sent with the simple return address of THE WHITE HOUSE, WASHINGTON, DC.

He considered his first cabinet: those he would select for personal loyalty; and the others for crucial Departments (State, Defense, Treasury) who must be first rate. Truman was remembered for the achievements of Acheson and Marshall, not his incompetent cronies who told dirty jokes. Beekman had learned from Tower's stories, and considered his future.

He was getting old and sentimental. But he would be good in the Justice Department: practicing law for the first time and watching for hints of corruption. Beekman smiled at the joke he would use to announce this appointment. Referring to when *young* Bobby Kennedy was appointed Attorney General by the president, his brother, "to get legal experience."

After stabbing out the cigarette he thought of LeeAnn and became saddened by the thought of what might have been. With his accomplishments overshadowing public discomfort with his divorce and very young second wife. Who was soon to be dead along with their child. This was something he regretted, for he cared about children and would not have permitted the virus to spread even if it insured his election. Well, *possibly* not.

The van's arson (likely by firecracker wielding delinquents no matter what the officials said) had produced the same effect: terror enough to sweep a man with his personality into the White House. Hire the best and grant them the freedom to succeed or else was his policy. And The Major was the best.

Tired by these reflections, Beekman fell asleep while mentally undressing his new nineteen year old aide. As LeeAnn and their son confronted readied guns.

BOOK FOUR

THE VENGEANCE OF THE LORD

Judgment, and Revelation

CHAPTER FIFTY FOUR

Tower had been to many such burials but he still felt awe. Flag draped caskets with union blue at their head, not permitted to touch the ground. Three rifle volleys. Taps.

Earlier, seated in church beside the First Lady, he considered the past week. Martial law had ended in New York City, just in time for the shopping season. Public relief at renewed triumph over barbarism. Excitement at next year's presidential election. The nation was again calm and prosperity reigned but all could have been so different.

The warmth of the packed church made him drowsy and he dozed. Until being aroused first by a nudge and then a smile from his companion, as her husband began speaking. He was startled to hear the words which *he* had suggested.

"'Depart from evil and do good. You have done wrong, then balance it and do right. If a man rises completely above sin and turns away from it absolutely then God, who is faithful, will not allow him to suffer for one moment. God is a God of the present and takes and receives you as you are.'

"These words were written eight hundred years ago by Master Eckhart and, the Bishop believes, are as true today.

"We are here to witness the tragedy of death and the triumph of good. To speak of those who will never fulfill their promise, yet will live forever in our memories, having sacrificed all for our nation. Can there be there greater patriotism or virtue?"

Tower covered his face as if he were mournful. But he grimaced as he remembered the night before their deaths. Having listened as The Major informed LeeAnn of their relationship. The Major's amendment to Tower's plan. Then Detroit shepherding David and Trixie (an odd nickname, Tower thought, for one so subdued) to her apartment while the others left New York City.

Dalling driving, dressed in his old colonel's uniform. The Major, wearing squadron leader insignia and holding British documents, accompanying his alleged American wife and newborn to a motel in Orange County. They flying the next morning on a C5-A transport ferrying supplies from nearby Stewart Field to Bosnia with the plane being unexpectedly ordered to stop first at a base in Northern Ireland, a short drive from The Major's home.

And Tower's promises to David and Trixie: funds for David's psychiatric residency and psychoanalytic training in exchange for he accepting an immediate military commission; and a scholarship and early admission for

Trixie into the joint College/Medical School program at The City University.

With hints of trouble were they to gossip: reassignment to Guam, and the State Medical Board learning of David's harboring and treatment of a minor; and the Family Court of Trixie's dangerous chemical experiments. Threats which were hardly necessary with such enticing rewards.

Tower thought that gaining these would demand all of the favors he still held. But the president quickly agreed once he recognized the effect on his re-election prospects.

So by 1:10 A.M. the assault on the empty apartment ended. Several hours later following the receipt of Tower's information and suggestion, LeeAnn's parents and Beekman sought her within the concealed storeroom.

Tower imagined him fondling the switch hidden within the plaster vagina. The chamber's entrance opening and then closing. Seconds later, the explosion of *hellhounds* left by those despicable terrorists who had kidnapped and held LeeAnn captive. But freeing her after childbirth, recoiling from the unfavorable publicity her murder would arouse. Mother and baby were now safe and recuperating abroad.

Burial in Arlington National Cemetery for Beekman, a National Guard (six month active service) veteran, and LeeAnn's stepfather, who briefly served as State Department Chief of Mission thus becoming eligible for interment there together with his wife.

"There is work and good works," the president continued. "Beekman did both. His concern for children was reflected in his speeches which *revered* them as being the promise of our nation. *And by his final act*: rising from a sickbed to save a desperate child" (this was another line which Tower suggested).

"Thus I will sign legislation appropriating funds for one Ralph Beekman Residence for Adolescent Mothers in every state. With two hundred fifty million dollars matching funds to counsel troubled youth. A lasting tribute to those we honor, of whom little remain except—*him*."

Into the hush and tears the president reached under the lectern and raised a wounded figure: limb torn, foot charred, its name sash was faded though still resplendent: **DEVONMERE**.

CHAPTER FIFTY FIVE

LeeAnn was ready to chuck being a mother. Like last night when she was woken at 11:30 P.M., 2:10 A.M., 4:15 A.M., and 7:12 A.M. Between watching, changing, breast-feeding, and playing with her son, pumping herself for when she felt too exhausted to move, *and* caring for The Monsters, she longed for her relaxed high school days.

Her brother wasn't any help. Not that he didn't love Thomas (named after their father). But he was clueless how to play with a baby or even knew that children needed toys. Though he was starting to learn after her sisters drove him crazy to buy them some. Mostly he just moped and tried thinking up more ways to protect them.

Two retired armed detectives accompanied them everywhere. Grounds were floodlit at night and embedded with geophones which could distinguish between human and animal movement. Even the live-in cook/gardener couple carried guns, she had her own Baby Colt, and had started target practice in the basement. Talk about living on the frontier!

She hadn't yet gone into town. Her only friend, Father Brian, explained.

"Your brother led a perilous life. He fears both the joy you bring and losing it. Yesterday he spoke lines from Longfellow

> I HEARD a voice, that cried,
> "Balder the Beautiful
> Is dead, is dead!"

I'll talk to him."

Which was how LeeAnn, her son, and her sisters came to be in Dundalk two days later. Accompanied by two middle-aged men who watched from an adjacent table while they lunched in a small tea shop.

The Monsters were doing better. They were less frantic and reading more, though they still cried for their MTV. They would have to attend school no matter the size of their brother's fears.

"Young for three," the waitress remarked, as she brought the bill.

"Just the baby's mine."

"A beauty," she cooed.

It was late afternoon and only they remained in the shop. Desperate for companionship, LeeAnn invited the waitress to join them.

While the pastry tray occupied her sisters, the women talked.

"Bridget," the shop girl introduced herself. "You're Letitia, The Major's sister."

"How did you know?" LeeAnn asked, liking the sound of her birth name and deciding that moment to adopt it.

"It's a small town. There's only one American here with kids."

"Stifling."

"Get to Dublin with your husband."

"He...died."

The silence lasted several moments.

"So did an old man I tended. Even with them it hurts."

"Nurse?"

"I'm a second year medical school student. My mother's shop pays for it and seven others."

"How old are they?"

"I'm the oldest. They're six, seven, nine, ten, twelve, fifteen, and seventeen."

A *real* family with playmates for her sisters, Letitia thought. She's smart and pretty. Big breasted like the other women her brother dated. The older sister she always wanted...

"Do you have a boyfriend?"

"They drink too much around here."

"My brother hardly touches it. Have you met?"

"I saw him. He's very good-looking. Rich too."

"But stingy. Look how I'm dressed. Come for dinner tomorrow. Early about six. You two can talk while I'm off breast feeding. Here's my number." She scribbled on a napkin. "Give me yours. Don't bother what to wear: he's the only formal one."

Bridget wrote, and the women smiled conspiratorially while dressing the children.

CHAPTER FIFTY SIX

TOWER CONSIDERED WHAT he knew about death and judgment. That Christians believe death resulted from sin which man, as originally created, was immune from. But they could be redeemed into a new life, if considered worthy after rigorous trial. Tower believed that his case was winnable if it were heard, and only God would.

He missed Beekman, though he had been a gravely flawed man. Despite his passion about America he had always remained ignorant of its essence. Tower loved him as the child he would never have and remained grateful for the family Beekman's had provided him.

Despite fervent and lengthy opposition from his Cabinet, the president agreed with Tower's insistence that The Major be chosen for the job. Tower wondered if only chance caused Letitia to call, even as he received the documents.

Though he was only a little less frightened of flying than driving, Tower had promised her to arrive in Ireland by the next day and did. At the airport he was met by a Range Rover containing Leticia, her baby, and thug look-a-likes he learned were ex-detectives.

Motherhood suited her, Tower thought. She was now more thoughtful and assured. While the luggage was being collected, she asked him to hold Thomas, as he first did on that terrible night of his birth.

Only after the car was moving and the window panel closed did her desperation reappear.

"I'm scared. He's depressed and has guns."

"Did he say anything?"

"He doesn't. Just gets up to eat, then lies on the couch all day. Though he never talked much at his best. And he totally ignores my girlfriend who would make him a great wife!"

Despite her pain, Tower couldn't help smiling.

The Major lay on a sofa, dressed in slacks and bathrobe, with an open book atop his stomach. Despite the presence of toys and the faint cries of children, the room seemed grim. Drapes were drawn, and a shotgun was beside him on the coffee table: an Italian military SPAS 15 which Tower recognized from a recent sales presentation/buffet at the Pentagon. With kids around he hoped that it wasn't loaded.

Tower sat and waited. Then he spoke softly.

"Letitia called me."

"Beware of saving a life lest you accept responsibility for it."

He waited more.

"Retirement to an Irish village isn't for you. You're bright and need dreams."

"Like Beekman?"

Tower considered whether to tell the truth, and then did. Feeling that with this action he was accepting a new commitment.

"I promised his father."

"That you'd make him president?"

"No, for he knew him too well. That his memory would be honored and it was."

More silence, but now a comfortable one.

"Why have you come?"

"To hire you."

"What country would have me?"

Tower didn't reply. Instead he reached into his briefcase and removed a manila envelope which he placed on the coffee table. Within, The Major found three documents. With less self-control he would have jolted upright at their sight. He was only a little less surprised at seeing his real name, which he hadn't used since leaving Devonmere.

Topmost, and signed by the American president, "pursuant to power conferred upon me by Article II, Section 2, of the Constitution, have granted and by these presents do grant a full, free, and absolute...for all offenses against the United States...committed or may have committed or taken part in during the period..." A pardon.

Beneath was a letter signed by the British Home Secretary which, if not exoneration, was close. Stating that injustice had occurred and "to do nothing would be neither compassionate nor humane," it asked that his childhood behavior be considered with "understanding, forgiveness, and wisdom."

The last document was extraordinary. Signed by the American general commanding SHAPE*, it stated that since The Major's twenty first birthday he had been employed by ACE**, which covers the area from Norway through Turkey. And asking that all police and military forces in the NATO countries assist and protect him.

Truly A Get Out Of Jail card!

Now Tower spoke his final words.

"Here (placing a smaller envelope on the coffee table) are tickets to Washington for you and your family. Pictures of a house in Annapolis rented for you, with good schools nearby and an easy commute to Washington. Call me when you get in."

Then he left to have dinner with Letitia before returning to America.

*Supreme Headquarters Allied Powers Europe
**Allied Command Europe

The Major lay on the sofa the rest of the evening, falling asleep and finding the letters on the floor when he woke. He noted that Tower had left them without learning his decision.

After locking them in the safe, he went for a walk but returned after a hundred feet. Astonished at having left the house without a pistol for the first time, and feeling freer with each step.

It was still early so he showered before going to Letitia's room. She was sleeping with the kids. Probably one had another nightmare. He sat and watched until she was roused by their movement. Then he opened the drapes.

"Is something wrong?" she asked.

"No longer," he replied with his first real smile that she had ever seen. "We're going...home."

EPILOGUE

June 2,

Dearest Bridget:

It's been months and I do really do apologize for not calling or writing but things were crazy. The house is OK and the kids are finally in school. *After* we got references from my brother's boss who they watch MTV with. Though the principal probably thought that a mother my age is just Valley trash with money.

I spend all day talking baby talk and GOING CRAZY. My brother is worse than my mother was at her worst. Then I didn't have guards following me.

I REALLY NEED YOU SOONEST. So does my brother who works all the time and won't let me date. Probably not till he's married!

Enclosed is a ticket to Washington. Even a return one in case things don't work out. It's in three weeks during your vacation. I checked with Johns Hopkins and you can finish med. school there without losing credit.

YOU HAVE TO COME! I bought these with the emergency house cash and they're nonrefundable so if you don't I'm in big trouble.

Thomas asked about you *twice* since we left and you know how uptight the English are so what that means. You'll stay in the room next to his and I won't see anything though I can't promise for The Monsters who always know everything. They PLEAD for you.

Don't bring anything. We'll be at the arrival gate and shop on the way home. With my budget money.

With Bestest Love from me,
The Monsters, and both Thomases,

L.

SELECT BIBLIOGRAPHY

BOOKS

Adams, Thomas K. *US Special Operations Forces in Action: The Challenge of Unconventional Warfare*. London: Frank Cass Publishers, 1998.

Bauer, Stephen. *At Ease in the White House: the Uninhibited Memoirs of a Presidential Social Aide*. New York: Carol Pub. Group, 1991.

Dewar, Michael. *Weapons & Equipment of Counter-Terrorism*. New York: Poole, Dorset, 1987.

Douglas, Joseph D. *America the Vulnerable: The Threat of Chemical and Biological Warfare*. Lexington, MA: Lexington Books, 1987.

Doyle, William. *Inside the Oval Office: the White House Tapes from FDR to Clinton*. New York: Kodansha International, 1999.

Follain, John. *Jackal: the Complete Story of the Legendary Terrorist, Carlos the Jackal*. New York: Arcade, 1998.

Ford, Gerald R. *Humor and the Presidency*. New York: Arbor House, 1987.

Hallswell, Michael J. *Herbal Healing: A Practical Introduction to Medicinal Herbs*. Garden City Park, NY: Avery, 1994.

Laqueur, Walter. *The Age of Terrorism*. Boston: Little, Brown, 1987.

Long, David E. *The Anatomy of Terrorism*. New York: Free Press, 1990.

Marquis, Susan L. *Unconventional Warfare*. Washington: Brookings Institution, 1997.

McCuen, Gary E. (ed.). *Biological Terrorism & Weapons of Mass Destruction*. Hudson, WI: G. E. McCuen Publications, 1999.

Pemberton, William E. *Harry S. Truman: Fair Dealer and Cold Warrior*. Boston: Twayne, 1989.

Schapsmeier, Edward L. *Gerald L. Ford: Date With Destiny: A Political Biography*. New York: P. Lang, 1989.

Smith, Warner. *Covert Warrior: A Vietnam Memoir*. New York: Pocket Books, 1998.

Thomas, Helen. *Front Row at the White House: My Life and Times*. New York: Scribner, 1999.

Weidenfeld, Sheila Rabb. *First Lady: With the Fords at the White House*. New York: Putnam, 1979.

REPORTS

Canadian Security Intelligence Service. Reports on Chemical and CB Terrorism. 1997.

Johns Hopkins Division of Infectious Diseases, Johns Hopkins University. National Symposium on Medical and Public Health Response to Bioterrorism. *1997-1999.*

New Scientist. Bioterrorism Special Reports. May, 1996 - May, 1999.

United States Department of Justice. Report on the Availability of Bomb making Information for the United States House of Representatives and the United States Senate. April, 1997.

ARTICLES

Vandals Handbook (author unknown)

Cookbook: Thermite Incendiaries and Formulas (author unknown)

Excerpt from another great book by Stanley Goldstein

Park West: A Novel of Love and Murder
and Redemption

About *Park West*: A Jewish psychiatrist, haunted by guilt and recurring nightmares of the electric chair, dedicates his life to healing the poor before being accused of murdering women across America. Confronting certain execution, he prays for the first time: that his lover remain with him until his death. But the doctor has other allies: a lawyer seeking public sympathy; a retired presidential advisor to educate him on power and corruption; and a fallen minister who believes him Christlike, even, at times, the long awaited Messiah.

This rich, complex novel, bursting with characterizations of the successful yet lost, celebrates the power of love and redemption, and search for enduring values.

FOREWORD

DARLINGS,

I may be dead when you read this. Possibly your mother too. I wanted it this way, feeling that some events were too personal to share while we lived and still dangerous for you to know. As you might expect, *she* objected, so the final decision will be hers.

I began writing this as salvation. Later, after gaining answers, it became a story. Finally, just a life.

And like all lives it's fragmented, created from memories of events long gone. Except our love for you, always...

PREFACE

I NEVER LIKED lawyers: they charge too much, don't return phone calls, and have business practices which would cause the suspension of my medical license yet are ignored by their peers. So after my arrest I feared that mine would behave in these ways.

What should we handle first?I asked her. New York wants my medical license, the government froze my assets, and the Manhattan prosecutor is deciding whether he can arrange for my lethal injection more quickly than Texas or to let Alabama electrocute me."

Think, don't obsess, a psychoanalyst told me long ago. This being expanded on by my lawyer who advised me to "try to find some pattern in the events. Prosecutors can be wrong or even criminal but are never stupid."

So I now follow her advice and analyze my life believing, as I've told patients, that the unconscious knows what is crucial and will spontaneously raise it to awareness for deliberation. But I also knew the unconscious had no sense of time and I was running out of time.

Copyright © 2003 by Stanley Goldstein. All rights reserved.

Park West is available in a print edition now. It will be available in an E-book edition in early 2011.

www.ingramcontent.com/pod-product-compliance
Lightning Source LLC
Chambersburg PA
CBHW030910120626
46554CB00001B/83

9 7 8 0 9 7 1 7 7 0 5 1 5